M000013437

Off the Path

An Anthology of 21st Century Montana
American Indian Writers, Vol. 1

Edited by Adrian L. Jawort

Off the Path

Copyright © 2014 by Adrian L. Jawort

All rights reserved.

Printed in the United States of America

Published by:
Off the Pass Press LLC
2224 U.S. Highway 87 East #43
Billings, Mont. 59101
www.offthepasspressllc.com

All rights reserved. No part of this book may be reproduced or transmitted by any means without the permission of the individual authors.

ISBN-13: 978-0-615-96009-8
ISBN-10: 061596009X

All characters appearing in this work are fictitious. Any resemblance to real persons, living or dead, is purely coincidental.

All story's individual rights are reserved to the authors listed.

Cover photo by Tex Jawort

"I write in blood because I remember what it felt like to bleed."

~Sherman Alexie

Preface

It was the late and great Montana Blackfeet and Gros Ventre writer James Welch who said, "I think ethnic and regional labels are insulting to writers and really puts restrictions on them. People don't think your work is quite as universal." While Welch's stories of inner turmoil universally resonated with readers, it was writing about what he knew as an American Indian growing up on his ancestral and present day territory that ultimately propelled him to literary eminence. Or as he noted, he "was a writer who happened to be an Indian, and who happened to write about Indians."

In my dozen or so years as a journalist, I've had the pleasure of speaking to a lot of American Indians who've left their reservations to pursue various successful endeavors. Their personal experiences had them wanting more of their own tribal people to explore the world outside of their reservation comfort zones and rural areas in that they'd also be able to expand their own horizons and seemingly constricted viewpoints.

While living at home, they didn't believe their observations, insights, or even hardships counted to the rest of an indifferent world; but while away from it they experienced revelations about how truly unique their homeland is, as other people were truly fascinated and yearned to hear more about the area they came from.

And although some of these fiction stories aren't even necessarily about American Indians, this anthology will nonetheless open a portal into that world as told from one living in the 21st Century—because it is a unique viewpoint. For those of you who do know these places and feel these characters from your own personal trials and tribulations, I hope this helps tells your story as well. For those of you unsure, I cordially invite you to hop on this war pony of life and take a ride to a place you've never been.

And of course, special thanks to the contributors who made this anthology possible, and I hope many more successful ones like it are in store for years to come.

~Adrian L. Jawort, Northern Cheyenne

CONTENTS

God's Plan

By Cinnamon Spear

First to awaken, I observe how the light of summer's dawn has a dominant presence in the room ahead. *I wonder what the sun sees.* She's never around for the worst of it, shining tender light on the little white house with green shutters placed among gentle hills of the prairie. *Does she see a peaceful house? A pleasant home?* As I tiptoe down the hallway, I'm hesitant but ready for what I may or may not find. The lighting alone leads me to believe mother's curtains were torn down again.

Mom, the Queen of Improvisation, has mastered the unique art of tactfully picking over yard sales for rugs, throws, pillows, candles, lamp shades, anything that will match the color scheme of her choosing. She spends her days learning from home-improvement shows, though I know her favorites are Cake Boss, Iron Chef, and Rachael Rae. Of course they use knife sets and appliances that are worth more than our family's monthly earnings, so she can only make do with what we have; and she does. Dad never seems to celebrate her findings when she hits gold. He falls far from appreciating her eye for a bargain, because to him she isn't mimicking *feng shui* strategists or interior designers' furniture layouts; all she's doing is spending the little money he makes as a part-time legal advocate for the people in the county court.

I saw him in action one time. He was good. He was *really* good. Custody battle over three kids; he defended the mother and argued the father was an "unfit parent" because he drank and threw a boot at his 3-year-old son once when angry. I couldn't believe it. He was so quick with it, confident, and even had to explain parts of the legal code to the under-qualified judge! I sat stunned, in awe of my dad. I was almost proud of him. I still can't quite wrap my head around the idea that one man has the right to tell the next that he's not fit to be a parent. *Walk in the courtroom a dad, come out with no kids?* I wonder exactly how much Dad hated his job *that* day. I couldn't look him in the eyes for a while. Of course he won the case for the lady; he's said ten million times he'd be an attorney by now if it wasn't for mom. I mean, yes, seven years ago she lost the baby, but they were *both* doing drugs. (White powder and mirrors aren't easy to hide.)

Feeling like a paratrooper going into the fray once more but not knowing whether or not the chute is there, my heart is turbulent in the silence of the house. Any calm that exists here is always a degree closer to the stillness of death, than to the peace of tranquility. My role as older sister to three siblings inherently places eight tons of responsibility on my dainty 14 year old shoulders and kindly deferring, "No, thank you. I'll pass," is not an option. Millions of other American children are in their pajamas carelessly enjoying the aroma of blueberry pancakes while watching Saturday morning cartoons on CBS, yet here I am in East Bumfuck, Wyoming unknowingly prepared to practice real life First Responder EMS training in my living room. I continue down the hallway carrying caution in one hand and stealth in the other.

Halfway there, I close my eyes and stand still using my sense of hearing to determine the scenario that remains waiting to be discovered. *TV's off.* Can't hear the birds chirping or the rustling of the cottonwood leaves from the tree that stands tall in our front yard. *Door's shut.* I listen closer to hear the sound of tires along the red shale driveway that leads to the house from the highway. *No one's pullin' in.* My ears shift focus from right to left to assess the kitchen and for some reason my eyeballs, behind closed lids, also swing that direction. *Nope, nothing, kitchen's empty.*

Back to the room ahead of me, there is no sound of air forcefully working its way in and out of the lungs, teeth, lips of an obese individual unconscious due to alcohol intake. There is no sound of thick saliva and unswallowed bits of food being jostled in the esophagus of one who has passed out on the couch with his or her head hanging straight back. There is no sound of a vehicle without a muffler idling in the driveway or anyone making their way up the concrete steps. *Coast is clear.* First and foremost, I look out the big picture window past the leaves of the chokecherry bush to see if the brown GMC Safari van with a red hood is in the driveway, as is routine on a morning such as this. *They're in the house.*

The curtain rod is still connected on one end but touching the floor on the other, which proved my hypothesis.

Off the Path

Curtains: completely down, not just open. Evaluation of sunlight on the wall: correct. I smile. *I'm gettin' good.*

Friday night tornadoes have touched down for as long as I can remember, and they always leave a beautiful mess for me and my sisters to clean—though there remains a longstanding debate over whether it's worth cleaning because more often than not Saturday and Sunday night bring similar catastrophes. Amidst the familiar stench of bitter staleness and belligerence, sit two half-eaten, dried out hamburger sandwiches on separate plates, both Dad's. Mom never eats while drinking. The chips that I assume accompanied those meals are crushed into the carpet. A few pizza crusts are strewn about, one on the coffee table, others on the floor. Both lamps were knocked over but after careful examination, I am happy to find that they still work, the shades just needed to be reshaped. "The King of Beers" tends to expand his reign over our living room more often than I would like. His Majesty claims territory with eighteen to thirty-six dented, half-full, crushed, empty cans. There aren't any clothes this time, which is nice. I don't particularly *enjoy* having to touch bras, boxers, or anything covered in cum, blood, or beer.

I always like to clean according to content because it almost feels like a game when I do it that way. Broken glass, furniture, dishes, cans, clothes, trash. I scan the room high and low, imagining Budweiser cans to be Easter eggs when I hear footsteps down the hallway. Breathing in quick, I hold air and shoot my eyes towards the hallway, *heavy or light?* Definitely heavy. Temporarily paralyzed, I evaluate. *Mom or*

Off the Path

Dad?

Shit! Dad!

Fight-or-flight response kicks in and I panic. There is nowhere for me to escape, except into the kitchen but he'll see me pass by if I run that way. I can't disappear behind the couch because I'll have to come out sooner or later. My heartbeat climbs through my throat, into my cheeks and almost makes it to my eyes before I realize I haven't yet replaced the curtain rod and I'm casting a shadow.

It's too late to hide.

All I can do at this point is take the bull by the horns, assuming it will be a bull to round the corner. No one ever knows what spirit to expect in Dad, the morning after. Some days he'll wake up the same blood vein-bulging, raging lunatic from the night before. Some days he'll wake up being the soft-spoken nice guy who wants to take the kids fishing. My face becomes flush and I inhale to prepare myself for the unknown.

"Whoa," he says startled, staggering backwards a few inches, blinking hard to shake the sleep from him eyes. Obviously he paid nowhere near as much attention to his surroundings as I did before entering the room. He didn't even catch my shadow. He manages, "Hey-y-y, sweetie," with a cockeyed, crooked smile before a belch broke loose.

This was not the bull. But this also was not the clean-cut suited man who leaves in the morning and walks in around 5:15pm saying, "Whadda day, whadda day" with an exhale and a head shake. This was also not the man who

11

drives Cheyenne Avenue lifting a finger to suggest a wave as each car passes. This was also not the man to whom upstanding people in town nod their head to from afar. Nor was it the man that cannot go to the store or post office without someone stopping to tell him their problems. This was a sleepy grizzly fresh out of hibernation.

The pet name "sweetie" left his mouth and danced dark circles around me. I cringe, similar to when you come into the kitchen and you're the first to find a mouse dead in a trap. *Sweetie? Really?* The affection he attempted to send with those two syllables was met, doubled, with disgust. His eyes, glossed over, seem lost in a haze which doesn't quite seem possible compared to last night when they were targeted so strictly, fuming with fury.

Elizabeth, just two years younger than me, has perfected the art of turning herself invisible. She can do it even as she stands right in front of him! I secretly resent her for never being forced to endure his wrath. Too often I'm the one submitted to the spotlight of suffering associated with those evil eyes and the only way to get them off of you is to do or say something that will direct them towards someone else. As the eldest, I feel like it's my place to protect the others so I never resort to pettiness to save myself. From time to time, I even willingly throw myself into the line of fire by starting an argument with him to ensure Mom lives to see morning.

My heart used to break at every scene of fighting that played out before me. I could only imagine how much it would hurt to be hit with full force by my dad in his maniac stage.

Off the Path

When I was seven, I justified the pain Mom endured with the following logic: Dad's a big person and Mom's a big person. They're the same size. Elizabeth and I are the same size. It doesn't really hurt when Elizabeth hits me. Therefore, it must not really hurt Mom to be hit by Dad.

One time, I walked down the same hallway that rattled with the echoes of his shouting. "Get the fuck up, bitch!" He hollered at my mom from the top of his lungs. I could care less for how loud he could get with his nonsense; my concern lay in the fact that Mom's screams had silenced this Christmas night.

"Get the fuck up, you slut fucking bitch!"

I came quickly around the corner and paused upon entering the living room having found, not presents, but my mother's body slumped on the cold white tile floor in a pool of dark red blood, as naked as the day she arrived on this earth. My dad stood above her with his over-grown buzz cut dripping sweat and a torn shirt decorating his plump frame.

"Da-a-a-ad!"

"Ahh, she's alright. She's just faking." He swiftly kicks her twice in the stomach, "Arentch'ya, bitch? Get up, you dumb slut whore!"

She didn't even flinch. I had *hope* though, because sometimes she plays possum and keeps her mouth shut, taking massive blows to the head with her teeth clenched together until they come close to cracking, while tears escape from closed eyelids. She can withstand physical torture like no other and she bears the bruises, scratches, and bite marks like a warrior. She wears sunglasses and extra cover-up in public but can't fully hide it from the cashier in the store or the lady at the post office. Gossip runs like a river through our tiny town of 1,800. Anyone who hasn't seen has surely *heard* that my dad is an abusive drunk. But he's one of the most educated, feared men around so they let their eyes do the talking while they say nothing. Even my uncles who are bigger than him are afraid of him. *Pathetic fools.* Mom stays with him for the kids, or because she has no money of her own. Either way, she is undoubtedly the strongest and the weakest woman I know, rolled in to one.

I ran to the left of the Christmas tree and kneeled at his feet undisturbed by the fact that my mother's nipples and pubic hair were entirely exposed just feet from me. Nudity and carnage seemed to be frequent guests of the house, even during the holidays. Martyring myself to shield her, I threw my fragile seventy-six-pound body over hers and held my defense until my dad accepted the message and backed away a step or two. I was lucky this time; there were instances I accidentally turned invisible when I would much rather have liked to be seen, assuming my dad would never willingly hit me. After being on the receiving end of just one of his sloppy punches, I knew there were major flaws in my it-doesn't-really-hurt logic.

I sat up, holding her cold face in my hands for a moment.

"Dad, you *KI-I-I-LLED* her!"

We were covered in her blood. Frantically, I screamed

at the highest pitch my vocal cords would allow, "You ki-i-i-lled her!" I looked at my dad hoping the bastard was reacting to the truth I just revealed to his drunken ass but the only thing my attention could focus on was a single drop of sweat, reflecting the lights of the tree, that departed his brow and remained suspended in mid-air...

"Good morning, my girl," his voice brought me back to the present moment as if every letter of every word from him took on its own personality and aligned to taunt me. That smile of his was sickening and I knew if I were standing any closer to him, I would be bombarded with his reeking halitosis. We were both standing in the semi-soiled living room but it was clear that I was the only one standing amidst memories of the events from the night before. I slowly let my guard down, understanding he wasn't in attack mode. I silently continued to clean and the repetitious cycle of internal debate began. No matter which Dad I wake up to in the morning, one fact always rang true: He didn't remember.

Last night, I gave up on God. It had been nearly a year since my Bible Camp counselor from Trail's End Ranch in Ekalaka, Montana had told me to pray when my parents fought. She told me to ask God to send angels down from the heavens. She promised that angels would come wrap their arms around my mother, use their wings as a barrier, and she would feel no pain. Like many nights before, I had my siblings circled in the room farthest from where my parents were going rounds. The four of us were on our knees, holding hands, heads to the floor.

Off the Path

As captain to the *Boat of Hope*, I began, "Dear Lord, put angels around Mom."

My siblings climbed aboard, "Let their wings be strong. Dear Lord, put angels around Mom..."

We sang that song like a lullaby. Whether innocent or ignorant, it helped *us* through times like these. However, last night, my ears could not deny mother's cries—she *felt pain*. The prayer continued to flow from my mouth but the meaning of the words suddenly disappeared. Held in secret from the crew, my devotion melted to disbelief. There were no angels. There was no God. It was all bullshit.

After having relinquished my faith, I was commanded to bring my two sisters and baby brother into their bedroom. "Getch'your asses in here—all of you." We marched in single-file, arranged ourselves abreast in front of him, and stood at attention like the little army we were trained to be. He sat in the armchair in the corner of the room and my mom appeared to be recovering from one of his choke sessions. He liked to lay on top of her, using all his weight to smash her mangled body underneath him, and press his forearm firmly under her jaw or just on top of her face altogether if he felt like it. Grabbing my 4-year-old brother by the hand, he placed him on his left knee as he began to sob. "Your mother and I are getting a divorce," he said with his head hung low. Next, for us came The Choice.

"I'm taking Junior. If you want to come with us, take a step this way. If you want to stay with your slut of a mother, then just stand there," he ended his weep with the growl of a lion that caused my hairs to stand on end. "It's okay," he sniffled, "if you don't want to come with me."

His tears were contagious and my siblings, struck by fear, stood hand-in-hand.

Looking over my shoulder, I saw my mom, slouched on the bed, hair matted and reaching out in different directions. Her glasses were lost, or broken. Her face was slightly distorted and swollen in places. Her eyes flashed back and forth between looking empty and having seen too much. Her entire being silently hummed a melody of numbness. My youngest sister was taken by my dad's tears and was the first to step his way. Elizabeth and I stood in solidarity and watched her walk until she was comfortably crying under my dad's right arm. He gently placed a kiss on her cheek and told her he loved her, which only caused us to cry harder.

"C'mon Elizabeth," he pleaded, "you can come." My sister looked me solidly in the eyes, through her tears, for a moment or two then slipped her hand away as she went to join the rest of the family. My body shuddered under intense pressure and it seemed because my decision came last, it was the most important. My mom had me at 22. I've always been her right hand but I was also the leader of the pack. The Gemini twins inside me ran full blast in opposite directions but came crashing back together causing my insides to be twisted and torn. A million thoughts ran through my head as I tried to outweigh the consequences of each option before me. My mom was a grown woman and my siblings needed me but they, at least, had each other and I couldn't leave my mom alone. The seconds had slowed to a crawl and it was as if I could hear the tears of every person I loved hit the ground. But the ones behind me, without a doubt, resonated loudest. I took a step backwards and the immediate expressions of abandonment and betrayal that splashed across my sisters' faces carved an unforgettable, distinct pain in my ugly heart. *How could I do this to my sisters?* They hated me in that moment, the kind of hate that even once forgiven never fully relinquishes. I know they hated me and I hated him for putting me in this position and I swore I would never ever forgive him for as long as I lived.

He stood in the morning light and replaced the curtain rod. "I said good morning, my girl. Did you sleep well?" he asked with a gentle voice that took all night to travel the world and find its way to him. "Hey! Go wake up your mom and sisters, huh? Today looks like a great day to go fishing."

He Doesn't Know He's Dead Yet

By Adrian L. Jawort

My brother is dead. He just doesn't know it yet. Tonight I think I'll tell him.

The sound of a wailing, bereaved mother over the death of her youngest baby son is the most beautifully ugly sound a human being can make. It's only beautiful because through that anguish we know the true love they lived. And it's ugly because while the unabashed noise that comes out certainly conveys a plethora of descriptive words, it most genuinely captures the meaning of true heartfelt pain as the mother who carried and cared so much for her baby that she'd die for them without hesitation only wants to trade places.

It's a terrifying, lonely, and angry experience because although humans are idly trained to tell ourselves the death of a loved one means they're 'in a better place,' we truly don't know where they are as words like 'heaven' suddenly ring as believable as Zeus living on Mount Olympus. We just know they're simply no more as the fresh hole in our heart hits us hard with a hollow realization we'll never hear their voice, feel their warm touch, or share fresh feelings of emotional affection together ever again. Everything we had together will be held by a thread of strong memory we hope will not eventually fade with time as we supposedly get better at the grieving process. All we want more than anything is to hug them after we see them walk into a room and warmly greet us, not say goodbye and hold their cold unresponsive hand.

And so it was as I went to meet up with my brother on the way to the local tavern. Or, "The bah!" he liked to say in a mock New England accent.

It was dreary cold that day, but the wind had died down and a fresh coat of shimmering cold snow covered the former blandness of the dirty, ice-covered streets, seemingly marking it as a new beginning. I stopped to zip up my jacket, then paused to appreciate the big flakes above me that fell, giving off an aura of Christmas. It was the end of January, and much to my girlfriend's dismay I'd been meeting up with my brother several times a week on this walk in the month. Lately, late at night he'd also show up and come visit me in my apartment to check on me. She'd caught me the previous week talking away to him. She passed it off as drunk behavior and tiredly told me to go to bed. Or I hope she did. The following morning she said she was worried because she heard me distinctly responding to someone and joking around, and asked if I needed counseling. I said I'd look into it.

"Hey," my brother said, looking to see what I was staring at in the sky. "Nice out. Looks like Christmas! Remember when we used to go out every time there was fresh snow to play football? It was basically just 'smear the queer' though?"

"We still do," I said. "But I just thought that: 'it looks

like Christmas!' But yeah we did it like twice in the last year! Played football. The one time with a beer can when we were drunk after the first heavy snow."

"Oh, yeah!" He smiled his famous smile. Our grandpa used to call him Smiley he liked to grin so much. One could call it 'shit eating' when you were annoyed with him, however. He was dressed in his usual dapper clothes. It wasn't an Armani suite and tie, but let's just say he wouldn't pay for a pair of pants or sweater unless it came with at least around a $100 price tag. Even his work construction clothes had to be the most expensive ones. Contrast that to me who went immediately to the clearance racks when I went to a chain department store to shop.

Not wanting to break the snowy mood that brought us closer, we walked silently the next few short blocks as the sound of scrunching beneath our feet was the only noise along with the occasional car driving past. I looked at our feet and did appreciate the fact my brother taught me the value of a good pair of hiking boots. With our $200 pair of Italian hiking boots—I got mine on sale for a little less, of course—you not only rarely slipped, they were more comfortable than any sneakers.

We walked in and stomped our expensive boots before heading to a dark back table for two, me grabbing a small bowl of popcorn on the way. I nervously waited for the bar maid to come, making small talk about football and the game highlights playing on tv, my brother listening casually before asking me about the New England Patriot's chances.

"Good, offense as always," I said. "But if their defense steps up..."

The barmaid showed up to take the order. "Do you need a menu tonight?"

"No thanks," I said. "Just a pitcher of 'Buttwiper' and two glasses."

"You mean 'Bud?' That's funny. I'll have to remember that! But two glasses?" she asked with a raised eyebrow. "You expecting someone? I can just bring it out when they come."

"Yeah," I said. "I mean, that's okay. Just bring it out now. Scratch that: make the second glass a Guinness."

My brother stared at me intently, oblivious to the lady who took our order, and sensed my apprehension. He said, "What's up? Something bothering you? How's the old lady treating ya? Is she mad about the other night drinking session and don't want you here? I don't blame her. You got to lay off the sauce, man. One thing to have a good time, another thing to let it be a motivation."

"I'm gonna lay off. Anyway, she's not mad about the other night," I said. "We were just talking quietly, I thought. Anyway, to be honest, I think she'd rather have me here tonight."

"What is it then?"

"Thanks," I said as the lady set the pitcher of beer and pint glasses down—the Guinness one in front of my brother. I poured myself a glass and waited for the foam to come down before slamming it. I filled it up again.

"Look, bro," my brother knew I was stalling. "You've

always been like the only one I can truly talk to about anything in the world. We're like practically twins because we're a year apart. If you can't talk to me, I don't know, dude. I guess...just fucking let it out. I love you, bro, no matter what."

"Alright. Just let me sip this one first. No major hurry. But you're right, I do need to talk to you about something. And I'm glad you feel that way. I don't know if it'll make it harder or easier. Both."

I slammed another gulp, and the beer had warmed me up a bit. That and the comradery of the stand up guy sitting across the table telling me I was the only one in the world he could truly talk to. Here he was, about the most popular guy in town with every other person lighting up at the mention of his name with something great to say about him. And there I was, a lonely sort and recluse who was dealing with depression and having trouble holding onto the very girlfriend who helped carry him through the toughest time of his life. I felt like a worthless human at times because I was tired of being a drag. Everyone needs someone, but I was becoming a completely broken person she was getting tired of trying to fix because she didn't have the tools. Only I did.

Nonetheless, with one of the most well-liked, upstanding, hardworking young men around saying what he said to me, it made me feel proud. To him, I was his personal hero who stood up to bullies as kids on his behalf; I was a positive role model writer and he was my biggest fan; and I was funny as hell and we had a thousand inside jokes. To the world I was drifting further away from reality—becoming a shell of what I once was—when I should have been getting 'better.' The world wasn't going to do me any favors, however, so I knew I'd have to fight through it to get back to being the me my brother knew and admired. I continued with a renewed confidence in that my brother would understand my decision.

"Alright," I took a deep breath. "How should I say this? Ever notice anything weird about us meeting up?"

"Not really," he said. "Same thing we've always done."

I didn't want to point out no one seemed to notice him, but actually a few people did—at least some of the time—and even acknowledged him. That at least made me not feel so schizophrenic, but at the same time this was obviously something way beyond that. I'd have to come straight out with it.

"Not that what we're doing is weird, but you, specifically," I said.

He gave a thoughtful look at what must have been my confused, fragmented looking self, before breaking into a classic 'Smily' smile. "Just say it, dude."

"I think maybe you do know, but I thought it rude to ask or tell you!" His continued, confidant, gleaming face was enough motivation and convincing to me he could handle it. I said it. "Anyway, you're dead, dude."

He nodded slowly. I didn't know if it was knowingly or if he was just taking it in. He said after a 10 second pause, "Um...yeah. How long?"

"About a year now."

His brow furrowed while ingesting the information. "Time flies when you're having fun, I guess."

"So you did know? Kinda, actually, sorta?"

He put his hand on his chin, took a deep breath, and nodded yes. "I knew, I think, but mostly I just didn't want to leave you. I don't know what's next, actually. I never saw any white light, I never saw any heaven or hell, I just knew sometimes I'd be hanging out with you like the old times like it was any other night; shooting the shit about politics or sports or wars or elections. Sorry if it caused you more grief. Or is it cool?"

I wanted to cry. A tear did come down and I wiped it. "It's way cool. I feel the same way. I don't want it to ever end: our never ending conversation about the fucking news cycle!" I chuckled to keep from crying. "Don't be sorry. I'm just scared now. I just feel something is supposed to happen now. I feel bad I have to even acknowledge it. But...I think I have to. Otherwise, you can't do whatever. And neither can I."

I choked out another tear before becoming paranoid of drawing attention from other patrons. No one noticed. I spoke again quietly to regain my composure. "Question: do you remember how it happened?"

He said, "Not really. How was it?"

"Oh, fuck," I said. The story made me angrier every time I told it, but he was the one person I could tell anything to with confidence, after all. "This will piss you off: you were murdered, dude. Shot and killed, and left to bleed to death by that asshole brother-in-law of yours."

"You fucking serious?" he said, shaking his head in disbelief while still somehow smiling about it. "Sum-m-m bitch. He said he wanted to do some target practice. I actually do remember that. Yeah, then he shoots me, I guess. It's coming back, unfortunately. Why did you be the bearer of this bad news? Just joking. Go on."

Him being chill about it was the nicest thing he could have done. "Yeah, dude, I thought you'd be more pissed."

"I am! That idiot moron of all people got me. The one guy I shouldn't have trusted. The guy is a pysho. I'm convinced he killed another guy before that. We all were down there. Anyway, yeah. Then what happened?"

"Well, I guess after he let you bleed out for a couple hours, he took you to the hospital when you were already dead. Claimed it was an accident."

What made me always mad enough to commit vigilante justice was imagining what really happened; my baby brother being blasted at close range by a high-powered rifle, unable to walk with a shattered pelvis as he begged some unsympathetic loser on a lonely, cold, Indian Reservation prairie to please take him to the IHS hospital before fading away. I would've blocked out that memory as well if those were my last moments.

"Really? And they believed him?" he said. "That it was an *accident*?"

"Well, no one does," I said. "But they don't have enough evidence to prove otherwise. But yeah he got sentenced a couple years for something lame like manslaughter."

"Fu-u-uck..." he said. "Well, he'll get his. No way that's gonna slide when he gets out! I just don't want you doing anything stupid, alright, bro? Don't ruin your life over that fucking ass hole. He's not worth the second thought. Anyway, what else is new?"

He laughed loudly. I had to join him a bit. I didn't care who saw me.

I continued on a more somber note. "I just...don't know why I didn't have the heart to tell you. I have a feeling for some reason we won't be seeing each other much now. I'll miss you, bad, bro. It's why I couldn't say anything before. I saw you come back to visit me and I just couldn't let it go either."

When the news of my brother's death came via cell phone, I was in shocked disbelief. Surely, there was some disinformation that had been conveyed. It was violent and they arrested someone? No way anyone would want to actually kill him. An auto accident would've been more plausible at least. I'd been on my way to the hospital to visit my sick mother, and when I got there I saw a Sheriff and Police Chaplain outside of her room talking. When I heard my mother's unrestrained crying, it erased any lingering doubts of his death.

For a month straight my body and mind drifted in shock. In short, I was a wreck, and all I wanted was for that sick feeling to go away. I noticed new white hairs on my head.

My heart constantly beat at a rapid and erratic rate as anxiety attacks I'd never experienced before completely rendered me in a useless tizzy to those around me so I spent most days hiding from the world. I avoided alcohol and other drugs lest they potentially make me flip out and grow crazier. Surely, murders happened to plenty of other young people before. Why was I so special that I couldn't all of a sudden function? What good was I to others like my mother who needed me to be strong, or my girlfriend who also had to suffer as she watched the one she loved fall apart day by day?

All I wanted was to not feel like a broken human on the verge of a complete nervous breakdown, so one weekend I embraced some sense of normality and took myself out on a date of sorts. I caught a bus and went to an afternoon matinee movie, and actually felt relaxed afterwards for the first time since I'd heard of my brother's death. At a restaurant, I decided to imbibe in some fine wine and a couple of beers, knowing I'd take a taxi home later. I tried thinking of the good times we had. I wondered what he'd think of the DiCaprio movie I'd just seen since it was one actually we'd agreed to go see together right before his passing. He would've loved it.

In the restaurant bathroom I washed my hands and face, looked into the mirror, and—for the first time in nearly a month—I genuinely smiled. Smiley would like it that way, I thought. I went out to my booth table and there he was, sitting across from my spot. He nodded with a wide grin.

We spoke as always. I even told him how bad ass the movie was, but I couldn't tell him the news of his death.

Afterward I'd see variably him maybe once every two weeks, or sometimes a couple of times a week. Nonetheless, I looked forward to our conversations. The anxiety attacks went away. I no longer privately thought I should get medicated with anti-psychotic drugs. I was working hard again and coming around, as they say. I could comfort my mother easier. And I only tried to 'conjure him,' so to speak, in absolute privacy.

But of course I wasn't truly okay, and I knew that deep down. I even theorized if he were a ghost, then he was so because I wasn't ready to let him go. It turned out I was right.

Regardless, I was torn in actually having to tell him he was dead versus not seeing him again save for memories. I couldn't blame him for looking out for me, but lately after our meetings I'd leave in shambles. I'd frequently drink out of sadness in hopes he'd come and see me again. But apart from rare occasions, he mostly wouldn't when I was too faded. I had to put it behind me to move forward. I wanted to live life, savor a beer, and smile like Ol' Smiley, not wallow in drunken stupors always hoping he'd come back.

So on the day before the anniversary of his death, I called my brother up one last time to tell him the news and have one final beer with him. All finished with my pitcher of beer, I grabbed the Guinness—his favorite lager—and saluted him with it before guzzling it down, enjoying every drop.

He said, "Just know that I'll always love you, brother. Also, thanks for helping me live such a memorable life and taking care of my baby son for me while I'm away. I know you'll be a good dad. And of course," he put on his jacket and switched his voice to a mock 'gentlemen' accent he was also fond of, "always a fine pleasure to imbibe in a drink our two and regale the tales of the past. But alas, I don't want to wear out my sojourn, and as such I'd better go forth."

"'Go forth' where?" I said.

"To home, I guess."

He gave one last mischievous smile, and went forth out the door.

Green-Eyed Regret

By Luella N. Brien

She lay on the concrete thinking she was cold. Cold was all she could think. The moon was high over her head, the stars covered by a thin layer of clouds. The blood matted her hair down, but all she could think of was how cold it was.

Uncommonly cold for May, the temperature hovered in the low 50s, but for the beginning of summer it just seemed too cold.

Yearning for a blanket, Maddy never made the connection that she was cold because of the excessive amount of blood she'd lost. She never quite realized that she was, indeed, dying. She lay on the sidewalk, her soul ready to make its final exit, but she was more preoccupied with the weather.

Exactly seventeen years after she was born, she was gone. As her spirit escaped towards the thin layer of clouds covering the stars, she became the statistic she never wanted to be.

***

Maddy grew up in rural Montana, where the cows far outnumbered the people. She spent her life an hour north of the Wyoming border, where the mountains met the sky and the air was *crisp and clean.*

She hated every minute of it. The tension between cowboys and Indians was palpable and Maddy never knew which side of the battle she was on. The tension permeated her blood.

In the hot August of 1989, her dad, a lanky rodeo cowboy with green eyes, competed at the Crow Fair Rodeo. He'd heard Indians made the best cowboys. Curious, he wanted to test that theory. Lucky for him it was one of the only years the rodeo was open to non-Natives. He was good in the arena, but his best performances were with the Indian women. He was pretty smooth. He told three different Indian women that weekend they were the "most beautiful Indian woman I've ever seen." He knew which ones to pick. He was never a fan of the prettier, arrogant girls. He liked the shy ones. They were easier targets.

But Maddy's soon-to-be-mother, Sydney, was different. She was outgoing, beautiful, and ready for anything. That personality made him leery. If she wasn't such an independent woman maybe he would've taken her with him, but he knew it'd never work. An Indian rodeo queen and a white cowboy? It just didn't seem like it'd be even plausible.

So he left with a bit of guilt, but it was nothing a few beers couldn't cure.

Sydney recalled it a bit differently.

She wanted to convince him to take her with him—she knew she could. She knew she had power over him, but he was an asshole and he smelled like cow shit. He was also one of the worst fucks she'd ever had. One of the other reasons she was so bitter about the green-eyed cowboy was not only was he a bad lay, he left her with a kid.

Nine months later Sydney, the most beautiful Crow Fair Rodeo Queen, gave birth to an 8-pound girl in the federally funded Crow/Northern Cheyenne Indian Health Service Hospital. Madeline Jean Thompson was born with green eyes and freckles. It was enough to make Sydney hate her baby instantly. She hated her so much that she gave her the lanky cowboy's last name.

Her life was ruined. Her dream of getting out was dead. Now she had a baby to tie her down. Sydney wasn't all that different from most of her friends, but her failure left an uglier taste in her mouth because of her potential.

Sydney gave the baby to her mother, and like most of her friends, she began drinking. She ignored the fact she had a kid, and if people didn't know better they thought Maddy was her kid sister.

Maddy spent the first 12 years of her life shuttling from her mom's house in Hardin—a border town right off the reservation—to her grandmother's nearly 40 miles away, close to the Wyoming border. She liked it out there. Even if it was a bit boring, it was calm. There was one road in and out. In the winter Maddy missed a lot of school because they'd get snowed in. They had a lot of fun on snow days.

Her grandma taught her how to do a lot of cool things. She made dresses, cookies, bread, and jewelry boxes to hold all the fancy jewelry she'd own one day when she was rich and famous. Grandma was the one person Maddy whole-heartedly trusted, because she knew she truly loved her. She never made her only grandchild feel bad for not being Indian enough; her mother did that all the time.

"Indian girls shouldn't have green eyes," her mother said every time she saw her.

Maddy couldn't find the strength to tell her mother it wasn't her fault she got knocked up by a low rent cowboy who couldn't hack it as a dad. Sydney had gone steeper downhill in the last few years after Maddy moved in full-time with her grandma.

After she'd done a line of meth with her cousin in the house and Maddy caught them, it was enough to be final. Maddy had put up with the men who came through the house lined up like her mom was a carnival ride. She put up with drinking; first it was just beer, then it was hard liquor.

But she didn't want to watch as the meth ate her mother away like she was a walking corpse.

Maddy was also glad she didn't have to see her mom drink Lysol. She'd heard she did that, too. Disgusting.

It went from bad to worse. People talked about Sydney like she was dead. In a way, the person she used to be was dead. People whispered about her mom's beauty like it was a ghost that haunted the town.

Sydney smelled like a toxic chemical combination of trailer park produced synthetic drugs and anti-bacterial spray. When Maddy knew it was only a short matter of time before Sydney died, she decided she wouldn't mourn her.

She never wanted to go back to her mom's place.

Off the Path

Sydney never made it a secret she didn't want her kid, and blamed all her failures on her Maddy.

Stretch marks; Maddy caused them.

No coffee; Maddy didn't buy any.

No toilet paper; Maddy used it.

No gas in the car; Maddy drove it up.

The sky is falling and the polar ice caps are melting; Maddy was sure she was to blame for it all. She even told everyone it was her daughter's fault she was a druggie.

Maddy couldn't quite figure out how having a baby could ruin someone's life 17 years later.

She wanted to be with her grandmother, and after her twelfth birthday Maddy was there permanently. Her grandma's house smelled like cedar, buckskin, and old cigarette smoke. It was strangely comforting.

Maddy dreamed of fame. She wanted to be the person everyone in town knew and hated because she got out, not the one they loathed because she had green eyes and freckles. She wanted more. Her last year of high school, which was dull and too easy for her, was fast approaching and all she could think of was how to become the person she dreamed of being.

***

Maddy had a boyfriend; she didn't like him very much.

He played football, which was a nice change because it seemed like Crow boys only wanted to play basketball. He only drank on the weekends and his parents were still actually married. For any other girl he was a catch.

He wrote sad, sad poetry about The Creator and owls or coyotes. He wanted to grow up to be a tribal chairman. It made Maddy want to gag.

But she kept telling herself he was a catch, and even if she couldn't stand his self-serving political dreams and stereotypical Indian poetry, she stayed with him. She smiled and played the part. Besides, the prom was coming up.

Maddy made her own dress. She had fun doing it, but hated the fact she was poor. If she had the choice she would have still made her dress, but she hated not having the choice. She never seemed to have any choices, except for one thing.

Sydney had a necklace that would work perfectly for prom night. It wasn't real gold, but it looked real. Her mom wore it when she was a rodeo queen. It was so perfect she decided to sneak into her mom's house and take it.

She wanted to ask Sydney to use it, but her mother was already convinced she'd come home from the prom knocked up. Maddy didn't want to have that conversation. She just wanted the necklace.

It wasn't the highest quality necklace, but it'd still be perfect. The chain was so fine she could barely see it when her mother had it on. The pendant was round, roughly the size of a nickel, and had a cluster of sparkling stones.

Maddy knew they weren't real diamonds; in fact, she was sure they weren't even cubic zirconium. Other people wouldn't know, and in the dimly-lit high school gym they would still shine like real diamonds.

It was exhausting being so angry and depressed all the

time. Maddy always tried to find happiness. But with a mother like Sydney and a deadbeat dad she never knew, Maddy's emotional state always turned to the worst case scenarios.

What Maddy wanted was one moment to be glorious—one moment to shine in her Podunk town.

It was easy to get into her mother's house since she never kept the door locked. But as easy as it should have been, it was still one of the most difficult things Maddy had ever done.

She was finally back in the house that was never really her home, and she didn't want to be there. It had been at least three years since she'd stepped foot in that place. But there'd be no big fight or emotional outbursts if she happened to see Sydney because Maddy had decided to burn that rickety emotional bridge.

Her mother didn't want her, and now Maddy didn't want her mother. It was as simple as that.

She knew her mom kept the necklace in a special jewelry box that was stashed under a floorboard. When she found the box it wasn't like she remembered it. It was just like her mother: the years had been unkind.

In it she found an old engagement ring, the necklace, and a matchbook as old as Maddy with a phone number written on it.

But Maddy didn't allow herself to care about the mystery contained in the box. The reservation was filled with mysteries that existed quietly. Besides, her mom's life had nothing to do with her anymore.

What would it be like if her mom did marry the mystery man who gave her that ring? The answer was inconsequential. Maddy figured Sydney would have made him miserable, too.

Maddy snatched the necklace and left quickly because just being in the house made her sick. The smell and the mess and knowing all what happened there—it was gross.

When she got back to her grandma's house she felt safe, warm, better.

Maddy found a gift waiting; her grandma had made her a crown of sorts. It was sweet of her. The head piece was made from the flowers that only grew at the foot of the mountains.

Maddy knew it would have taken her grandmother all morning to get out to the mountains. At that moment she felt more than loved and appreciated. Her grandma would do anything for her.

Maddy got dressed in her simple maroon gown with an empire waist and satin trim along the bottom. She was so proud of how it perfectly fit her. One of the benefits of being half white was having a small waist and real hips.

Maddy fixed her own hair. Her grandmother would have done it for her, but she wasn't home. Maddy was unsure where she was. She finished her make up and put her mother's necklace on.

She left her head piece on the bed when she heard the car horn impatiently honking and went outside.

Her boyfriend, who didn't rent a limo, came to pick

her up in his dad's Monte Carlo. He didn't vacuum it out, but he did wash the outside.

Maddy couldn't help think the car was like her life: clean and sparkly on the outside, a mess on the inside.

***

The dance was lame.

This was Maddy's third prom. She knew the first thing every couple did was get their picture taken.

The props were set up. Maddy thought of her stereotypical Indian poet boyfriend as just one of those props. His hair had product in it, his tux was lined up just right, and for a split second everything was like the Monte Carlo.

Maddy felt bad afterwards. She never wanted to hurt his feelings, but she knew she was. He'd either have to be a complete idiot or completely self-involved to not realize that she had no real feelings for him. She figured he was both.

Maddy began to wonder if she was capable of loving an optional person. Of course she loved her grandmother. She had to. She was the one who took her in, actually made her feel wanted, and gave her a place to call home.

But he was optional.

She wondered if he really loved her, even though he told her he did all the time. In fact, he told her too much. Maddy thought he was trying way too hard to get her to say it back.

He said it at the college and career fair.

"I love you."

She said, "Do you think the pizza they serve in the

cafeteria has real meat in it?"

He said it right before grand entry at opening night of Montana State University Billings powwow.

"I love you."

"Oh my gosh, did you hear about the chairman scandal?" she said trying to change the subject.

He said it in the hallway at school.

"I love you."

"Did you ever finish that math homework?" she said as she opened her locker.

Maddy didn't know how long she could keep dodging it.

He just didn't get it.

It was the prom, and everything and everyone told her that this was supposed to be one of the most exciting moments in her life, but all Maddy thought about was the disconnected relationship with her estranged drug addict mother as she stared downwards, hypnotized by the shiny necklace.

Could it have affected her ability to love the future chairman of the Crow Tribe?

Maddy got mad.

"I've found another reason to hate my mother."

The future political all-star thought she was talking to him.

"How could anyone hate their mother?" he said with one eyebrow was raised high, proving he was engaged yet confused.

"Huh? What are you talking about?" she muttered.

"What are *you* talking about?" he said, even more confused.

She laughed; he laughed, but he didn't know why he was laughing.

He thought they shared a comical moment. Maddy thought he was stupid. If he ever did become chairman the whole tribe would be screwed.

It's not like the dance was boring, but Maddy wasn't really into it. She was bored, and told her boyfriend she wanted to leave the dance and celebrate the night. He was shocked and excited, and assumed that meant getting drunk.

To Mr. Political it never meant having reckless teenage sex. It always meant getting shitfaced with his buddies and confessing stupid shit to Maddy—like how much he loved her.

That, of course, would make her gag.

***

Maddy's boyfriend got out of the car at the biggest beer haven just off the dry reservation.

The new building had become like that friendly whore everyone knew. They hated her because of who she was, but she always had what they wanted at cheap prices so they loved her.

The floors were never dry, and the pop cooler was less than half the size of the beer cooler. Winos always roamed the perimeter and would gladly buy alchohol for a couple of dollars.

Off the Path

Tired of waiting, Maddy got out of the car to smoke a cigarette and ended up wandering into the alley. She always felt the need to keep moving. If the car stopped she always got out and wandered around.

There was no real reason for her to wander down the alley. It was just her thing. She always did it.

The alley was dark and the night was busy. Maddy restlessly roamed around from side to side, but her boyfriend was taking too long. She was about three blocks down before she realized her necklace was gone.

She had to get it back. Even though she hated her mother, it still wasn't hers. She doubled back hunched over, and began the panicked search. Her boyfriend had begun a search of his own. He couldn't find Maddy.

He'd left the store with a case of beer, and started slamming a small plastic bottle of cheap vodka. He bought it the day before so he'd be able to get a head start on partying that night. His face contorted when he realized it tasted like rubbing alcohol. Up until this point he'd only drank beer. Beer was better than liquor, and he told himself as long as he drank beer he was a recreational drinker—not a drunk.

Tonight he didn't care. It was the prom, he was graduating soon, and he was getting tired of waiting. His friends were already waiting for him. He had to find the girl and take her home so he could go out and have some real fun.

Maddy was getting desperate; she was on her hands and knees frantically searching for the necklace. The one shiny pretty thing her mother owned. The one thing of her mother's that she ever wanted. She had to find it.

Her boyfriend drove down the alleys and around the neighborhood blocks, distracted by the CD player and his second vodka bottle. He drank the first one so fast the alcohol didn't hit him until half way through the second bottle. He reached for his CD case. Already swerving, he ran over a trash can, and decided that he was heading out before he couldn't drive anymore.

He noticed something on the floor.

It was Maddy's necklace. It was in the car, but she wasn't.

That girl's always doing something to piss me off.

He drove home. He figured he could give it back to her Monday morning at school.

***

Maddy was lying on the cold concrete. She'd fought her whole life against the idea she was nothing but trash, and on prom night her boyfriend thought she was. He didn't even look back to see if he'd really hit a trash can. He didn't think twice about it. He just drove onto a party while she lay dying on the cold concrete.

No one forgot her story. And in death she was finally famous.

Sweetheart

By Cinnamon Spear

He and I sat forehead-to-forehead completely getting lost in one another, communicating intensely through a shared gaze, no words. Nothing else mattered. The room, town, state, judgments of American society, human race fell silent. A deep fire in his Spanish eyes burned so bright it consumed my entire attention. I escaped this earthly compound while watching our love dance like a flame in the darkness of the night, stunned in a realm of thoughtless satisfaction. To delay being mesmerized forever, I'd lower my lids and disconnect eye contact. It was then that I'd have much to say, but the only way to get everything from me to him would be to open his heart and pour all of myself in.

Finally experiencing a closeness long desired, I rested my head upon his shoulder and he placed his gently atop mine. With closed eyes, and against the rules, I put my palm to his chest and felt the beat of his heart. I used everything in me to memorize the rhythms of his soul. I prayed to God and asked that from that moment forward, our hearts be synced so that no matter how much distance and time came between us, we forever hit every beat in unison ensuring that the love we have for one another continues to resonate on the same level and maintain the harmony we find between us now, into eternity.

In serene stillness, I reflected on the loves that I have experienced: the "I *think* I love you," the "I *wish* I loved you," the "I love you but I'm not *in love* with you," the "I *hate* that I love you,"—but never one as true as this. He is everything I hoped a soul mate would be and more. Tough but tender. Silly but serious. Unbelievable—but real. He saw the inner workings of my heart before he even laid eyes on me. He could finish my sentences before he ever heard my voice. My first words spoken to him were "I love you." Oddly enough, he didn't say it back. He had written it a million times, it baffled me that he didn't say it back. Didn't matter. He was a sweetheart.

Comfortably hand in hand, I giggled guiltily because I would have been in his arms, on his lap, probably making the most passionate intimate love ever if we were allowed even an ounce of privacy. I mean, he did subtly watch the "babysitters" (as we called them) like a hawk, snatching every possible opportunity to sneak me a kiss. I appreciated him for that. Nearly every one took my breath away, but I'm a *semi-exhibitionist* so it was definitely the fear of being caught that amplified the thrill every time our lips touched. I was curious as to how much more we could get away with. Just even his hand on my leg had me wanting him. Thoughts raced through my head like crazy but only one repeatedly made it out of my mouth.

"I love you."

"I love you, too," he said in a pointed way that left his lips puckered.

He had these deep, dark brown eyes and the longest eyelashes I've ever seen on a human being. He was rockin' his favorite haircut, "The Fade." He had smooth, unlabored hands, slightly clammy. My presence made him nervous. (I couldn't deny my heart rate was that of a humming bird's.) His build was similar to mine, long and slender, but not quite lanky or awkward looking and his skin was 10 shades darker brown than mine. If he had been outside more that summer he would have been drastically darker but I was almost thankful he wasn't.

"No, like, I *love* you, Love You, love you."

"I love you, too," he said in the exact same pointed way that left his lips puckered.

The sweetness of his love had me so addicted that I used the last week and a half of my vacation to road trip, alone, driving for 13 hours *straight*—just to get a taste. My green '99 Chevy Cavalier carried me across the rolling hills of Montana, through the badlands of North Dakota, and delivered me to the Land of 10,000 Lakes. The towering trees of the Minnesota landscape act as a security blanket for some and a claustrophobic cage to others. For me, they represented the heights of ecstasy that he provided. In between towns, I filled miles with thoughts of our similarities. Though he finished high school before I began, we would've been a force together, both active in cross-country, student council, community service projects and The National Honor Society.

His particular detail, witty humor, and free expression of self were all replicates of mine—all signs that we were created for one another. We existed, not as yin and yang, but as two reflective pieces of a whole, like each side of a heart that once brought together were complete.

Everyone that knew of my adventure ridiculed or lost respect for me. I appreciated those who disapproved in silence keeping their scrutiny to themselves and offered a piece of mind to those who didn't. It was all worth it in the end, I thought, and who are they to judge anyhow? Nobody's perfect.

"This isn't the kind of life you want," my dad sneered as he lifted the hood of my car. He knew I was going to follow my heart; the least he could do was check my engine before I left while voicing his opinion. "Not this type of guy."

"This *type*? What, the completely selfless type that showers a girl in love? Bwaha." I laughed, knowing my girl-talk-avoiding dad couldn't stomach the sweet stars in my eyes.

"Hand me that jug of oil, would ya?—I think what you're doing is pretty stupid."

"So. You and mom had years and *years* of being young and stupid. If this is my one weekend to be young and stupid, let me have it."

"But this isn't what you want."

"Everyone should just back the fuck up! No one can tell me what I want but *me*!"

I wanted him—that's all I knew. I made sure to be there at least 30 minutes early, each of the four days, so I was the first person let in. The more time together, the better.

There were vending machines but neither of us wanted anything. (I'm sure he thought I was too nervous to eat in front of him but hunger was the last thing on my mind.) Seven hours spanning breakfast and lunch but the only things we needed were each other, air, and maybe a little water. We were both quick talkers so we rotated bouts of non-stop stories with rounds of complete stillness and staring. The feelings we shared over paper only grew exponentially in person. After a day of nerves and warming up, we began to pick up on cues and mannerisms, each etching these cherished moments, facial expressions, giggles, whispers into our memory.

He needed his hands to talk. I noticed hesitation in his rendering of a story so I slipped my fingers out from between his, and off he went! Unspoken idiosyncrasies. Connection beyond belief. In one session of silence, he caressed my forearm with the slightest touch and in that minimal act, I felt whole. Staring aimlessly at the chair in front of me, I noticed how his up and down motion transformed into a repeating triangle. I shifted my attention to where his skin met mine. He was playing connect-the-dots with three freckles, one of which was so faint *I* hadn't even known it was there. He loved me gently, sweetly. A sincere touch my body had never before experienced.

"They'll tell you anything they think you want to hear," my mom warned, but I knew he was different. "That's what they do to keep you around." But I knew he would never deceive me. I could see his heart as clearly as he saw mine. He was my angel, surely as I was his. From his perspective, I quite literally fell straight out of the sky. *Michael, I know you don't know me but I've heard a lot about you....* My first letter was sent out into the big blue yonder. I didn't know what to expect as a response. I wasn't even sure I'd get one. Never in a million years would I have guessed the whim I took, bored in the wintertime, would have amounted in bringing me my other half. He was taken by it all too. "I'm amazed by how you came into my life just that short time ago, and you came right into my heart like you've been there before and you know the place...like you're *home!*" After 7 months and 70 exchanges, we were together.

"Count time!" hollered the man in the white shirt who looked like the overgrown bully from the playground of my youth, sounding annoyed to do his job.

There was an immediate shuffling and the room grew much louder. Michael's chair was closest to the wall, so I faced it and him. For the first time that day, I turned and saw exactly how many people were in the room. White families. Black families. Latino families. Indian families. Odd couples. Couples that looked like brother and sister. Old people. Young people. Children and babies. I wondered how in the world he captivated me so entirely that I hadn't even realized the extent of our company. I watched him join the others and I swear he didn't *feel* like number 12026-173. To me he wasn't.

To them he was. He might have been the knight in shining armor that told me, "If we only had one piece of bread and one glass of water, you would eat *and* drink before me," but to them he was 1 of 1,344 robotic sheep. He might have been the sweetest man I have ever met who responded to a story about my fingernail being halfway torn off with, "That must have sucked, going through what you went through. I'm sorry for you. I would have rather had that happen to me instead of you," but to them he was just another nameless other.

He stood across the room abreast with twenty or thirty guys, uniformly dressed. I scanned up and down the line knowing I wasn't alone when I wondered why are *they* here. He was a 27-year-old kingpin drug dealer that led an 8-year conspiracy to distribute cocaine and marijuana, currently 3 years into his 15-year federal prison sentence with 5-10 years supervised release and a $250,000 fine. But he was a sweetheart. He negotiated a non-cooperating plea agreement, "I did the crime. Give me the time," to ensure that the deserving or undeserving mother of his three beautiful daughters was granted immunity—therefore protecting her from any federal charges. He accepted full responsibility and testified against no one. He sat in holding, in County, and watched his closest friends roll over and over on each other. It was not his intent to hurt or help anyone. He lived off the thrill, loved being "The Man," and pushed all hours of the day and night to pump poison into the people, causing an impoverished community to deteriorate for nearly a decade. But he was a sweetheart.

The room became awfully quiet while the guards counted. Now more than ever, mental paradises deflated. The breath of imagination exhaled and exotic destinations were forced out of the women's heads. Instead, we sat staring at white cinderblock walls, gray plastic chairs, or straight down at our shoes in fear of catching the eyes of one another—for, we *chose* to be there. Once dismissed, the inmates dispersed themselves back amongst their loved ones. Couples used these precious seconds of mass movement to get in a kiss or cop a feel, knowing there was no way the guards could have their eyes on everyone at once. It was worth the risk. Even for us. The air settled and conversations picked up where they left off. Routine. It was *all* routine.

When the white shirt wearing man-child announced the end of visits, we rose to our feet. Like the gentleman he was, he handed me my clear plastic coin purse and bottle of water. Wrapping my arms around him, I put my head flat on his chest, listening again to the beat of his heart, committing his feel to memory, and enjoying his embrace. I looked up at him and we kissed. He pulled away and said, "You'll be okay," which filled my moment with confusion.

"Okay?" I wondered half baffled, "I *am* okay. I'll be back tomorrow, I'm golden!"

We kissed again and again, and quickly one more time. I loved the feel of his tongue against mine despite how, upon first meeting, they didn't dance quiet beautifully together. I knew we would achieve that in time. What mattered was that they touched. I was there. We were together.

"You'll be okay." He smiled half-heartedly, self-consciously, or all-knowingly.

I was okay. I was on cloud nine! I floated—blissfully—across the parking lot in a state of elation disregarding the 12-foot tall chain-link fence with barbed wire lining, easily ignoring the men whose eyes lay heavily on me as they walked circles upon endless circles around the track in the yard. I got in the car wearing a goofy smile and began to drive away while the twists and turns of Prison Road came between my body and my heart. In two days, I was going to return home, pack, and fly east for college but I was okay. I was a young, motivated, drug and alcohol free, "goody two shoes" kind of girl that never did as much as smoke a cigarette. I was the conqueror of peer pressure who had always preached against getting high or drunk thus working hard to escape a violent, poverty-stricken rural community myself. I innocently wrote a letter of support to a friend of a friend and fell insanely in love with a federally convicted father of three kids who was in prison for at least another decade. I was okay. *Wasn't I?*

He was my sweetheart.

Where Custer Last Slept

By Adrian L. Jawort

Come to think of it, no one outside his own circle really liked Tim that much. He'd always just been a spoiled, rich brat, bully all while growing up as far as we were concerned. His father was a temperamental but respectable hard-working man until he got some political power; then like many tribal politicians, he started hoarding all of the funds for his family's personal use. He would've been on his way to federal prison if he hadn't died so suddenly of a heart attack. I think the feds figured the book was closed on that case.

Someone else would take their turn hoarding the limited tribal finances, however, and soon you'd see relatives of theirs driving around in new pick-up trucks and SUVs.

One wonders if Tim wasn't such a brat as a kid, maybe we would've liked him better as he grew older and he wouldn't have lashed out so much. Probably not, as his ornery streaks always seemed to stem over the most trivial matters. All throughout school he never played sports—unless you call boxing other unwilling participants an athletic event.

That night though everyone liked Tim—he was especially rich. He had his inheritance from his father dying a few months prior, plus his newly acquired cattle grazing land lease money had conveniently arrived as well. He was quite the popular one with all the cases heaped upon cases of beer and a few liters of whiskey he'd bought. Tim himself walked around with a fifth in his hand of that god awful Lord Calvert whiskey. He was in a happy and as usual annoyingly boastful mood, but no one minded since his dad was dead. For the first time people sort of felt sorry for him—even me.

However, I still found it particularly irritating that Tim liked to blurt out obvious truths and act like the trivial motions someone was doing was somehow wrong.

"Ay-y-ye! This guy!" he'd yell really loud. "Really sitting there holding his beer and shit! Quit'chur babysittin'!"

Of course, said things like that supposedly passed as funny. The guy holding his beer would have to smile, nod, and be like, 'I guess,' lest risk unnecessary confrontation.

It was all harmless as long as you agreed with him, but show any disapproval and he'd try to pick a fight with you. This was fairly well known. Even people who didn't know him got those vibes off him, and they let it slide even when he was blatantly trying to start trouble since he was pretty buff. But damn that got old fast in a community as small as ours. We all had to build up some sort of shield to tolerate him. Aside from his two person clique, no one ever invited him to parties anymore. We knew he'd start shit every fucking time.

So there we were on some back road about five miles away from anywhere if you could call our 'rez towns' anywhere. This was the same area where George Armstrong Custer had camped before his last infamous day on the Little

Big Horn. The little towns were not so bad—Busby and Lame Deer. We complained all the time about having to live there, yes, but the towns themselves still had potential if the people started taking more pride in them, at least picked up the garbage that seemed constantly strewn about, and we maybe got some cell phone service and drinkable tap water. I'd love to see some big shot politician come and take a drink out of our faucets.

The immediate vicinity of Busby where I lived, population 936, aligned with the highway and looked like a miniaturized version of a 1950's box-style housing urban sprawl picture. In the background was a long hill with white sandstone that I thought always looked unique and haunting. The winding Rosebud Creek encased the other side of town. Steep, stout, jagged, and red rocked short mountains were a little bit further down the highway. That's the area where we were then, behind those red rocks on top of a long plateau. The rest of the general landscape resembled wooded miniature mountains that led to the town of Lame Deer, population 2,052. It was only a matter of time before a little kid finally got the match lit that finally burned most of those trees down. I remember when a kid my age used to always set grass fires to the prairies leading to the base of the hills until he got caught. Not surprisingly, his 10-year-old brother has followed in his pyromaniac ways. Although the kid brother was never formally charged, he'd been suspected of trying to burn down the school the previous year.

Nothing much happens here, so we were genuinely

grateful for Tim generously supplying us with the party, and appreciated it even more for the fact most of us were broke. We hardly get 'Indian money'—mineral rights per capita money or casino money—because we haven't sold out our land for it, and casinos are legal in this state already so there was no need for people to go out of their way to get to our very rural one. However, there was a rumor that we'd get a small $100 check in about a month. That passed for big news here.

Tim was actually very cool for the time being, and I was talking to my bro Eddie. He was going to the Army in the fall and was my best friend since infancy. Our moms were also very close friends since childhood, so Eddie's parents were also my Godparents. His parents basically adopted me into their family when I was little after my mom got sent to prison because my grandma was disabled and really couldn't fully care for my brother and I.

I wasn't Miss Popular or anything, but I did get along with almost everyone. My best female friend was actually my cousin Tara, and we were always together. We were all discussing our 'big future plans.'

"College, huh, Evalyn?" Eddy said as he finished his beer, crushed it, and threw it in the back of his little dinged-up, rusted, orange Datsun truck. He was referring to the fact I was going to the University of Montana—where I'd later decide to study journalism. He was the first person I'd elatedly told months ago about my acceptance. "I'm gonna go after the Army. I don't know what for yet, though. I might just stay in the Army forever. Beats this."

"Don't say that!" I said. "Four years is long enough. Hopefully I'll graduate by then...Hopefully!"

"Well then," Tara said. "Hopefully I'll have a plan by then. Hopefully! Ay-y-ye!"

Tara was pretty, petite, and girls (including me) sort of envied her for it. I mean, I know I was pretty, but a lot of people were still leery of me and said I was 'Gothic' since I did dress differently as far as rural Montana went with my modern rock and roll t-shirts, various piercings, and dyed hair. I know right? So shocking. Most popular rez kids were inclined to dress in the either contrasting western or hip hop clothes. Although Tara dressed very plain, she still looked like she could have been a super model she was so darn ravishing. She kept to herself though, and was disturbingly quite except around me. Most guys would talk to her briefly, get bored of her shying away, and leave her alone. They probably assumed she was stuck up. Even when she drank a lot, Tara hardly even raised her voice. She had problems at home that she rarely spoke of like her artist dad dying a couple of years earlier in an alcohol fueled car wreck, and she dropped out of school the previous year. Of course dropping out is dumb, but that's the norm around here. Hell, only about half of the kids at this party were even on course to graduating or had graduated last month, and it was a supposed high school graduation party. There was no one there older than twenty, except someone's two uncles that were buyers who'd made it clear they'd leave soon as soon as they slammed some of their share. They didn't want to get caught contributing to minors on a 'dry rez' where alcohol was strictly prohibited. It was a 'straight to jail do not pass go' offense—or at the very least a trip to the drunk tank for 8 hours.

My aforementioned soon to be college roommate came up to us and put her arm around me. "Was up, home girl Eva?" she staggered into me semi-purposely. "Ready to party or what in Missoula this fall?"

"Hell yeah!" I said. "No more high school. This is graduating to the big time of drinking!"

"Ay-y-ye!" us girls said in unison.

We both gave each other 'cheers' and she went to make her rounds elsewhere.

"I can't believe Gillian's gonna be your roommate," Tara said. "Well, at least she's friendly."

"A little too friendly! Sarah's gonna kill her," Eddy pointed with his lips and we saw her nudging her elbow against Tim. It was just friendly teasing though to the man in charge for the hour since everyone knew Tim was already hooked-up with Sarah—a girl even meaner than he was who lived in Lame Deer. It's like Tim and Sarah were meant for each other they were both so distempered, but she did keep him in line a little. Everyone was more scared of her than Tim, because at least Tim was fairly predictable. Sarah was not around on this night though.

The red blanket warming the earth stemming from the setting sun in the western sky was turning violet as it grew darker by the second. Before we knew it in our little happy drunken stupors it was black out aside from the half-moon and stars, but they gave off a decent fluorescence in the open field. For some of the remaining dozen or so guests that meant looking back at the stars, relaxing, chilling out, and swapping recycled stories. For others like Tim and his posse, that meant yelling around with their so called 'war whoops' or whatever at the sky. It was all in good fun though, as even Eddie was howling around. That's like a must for young males in the middle of nowhere when everyone is drunk.

The air was cool and serene. The sky was clear. These things I distinctly remember. I've studied the constellations as they've always captivated me. Faded...I got up off the tailgate and finally thanked Tim for the beer.

"No problem, you're my home girl," he said. Not really. "Congratulations though for graduating."

I told him, *"Nea'ese,"* (thank you). "You too. Congratulations," and I gave him 'cheers' with my beer can to his half-empty whiskey bottle.

I went back to the tailgate it was just the same 'ol same 'ol conversations for a long while with car stereos playing various tunes. It must have been around 1:30 in the morning before most of the cars left. Then there were seven of us: Me, Tara, Eddie, Tim and his two friends; and also a young cousin of Tim's named Bryce. Bryce was half Crow and half Cheyenne, but we didn't know much about him otherwise.

About a half-hour later a scuffle broke out between Tim's friend Cecil and Bryce. I suppose Bryce should have been immune from having to fight since he was invited by the host Tim, but that didn't matter. Tim was no help, as he was the main one urging the fight on. The skinny but tall Bryce only looked like he was about fifteen and was way over matched in bulk and kept backing away.

Cecil lunged and connected on a punch, but Bryce managed to block most of it and push him from the back after sidestepping him. Cecil fell hard on his chest with his momentum. He got up, rattled and embarrassed as his friends laughed. This made him more aggressive and determined.

"What the fuck, man?" Bryce was yelling and jogging backwards, avoiding the drunken Cecil like a matador does to a bull. "I said I don't wanna fight! I didn't even do shit!"

Tim and his other friend Keith continued laughing and drinking. I suppose it was funny in a way, watching the large, oafish Cecil stagger around until he'd inevitably trip over some sagebrush. Tim went behind Bryce in an effort to make him stay in a spot so he'd be forced to stand his ground. I'd gotten closer to the action by then and I saw the look in Bryce's eyes: a scared, drunken child desperately trying to make sense of the situation. Tim shoved Bryce into Cecil and a flurry of punches ensued after they both fell to the ground.

Bryce rolled away before Cecil could get the best of him and stood up. His eyes were searching frantically for the help or support that would never come.

"Get in there, you little bitch!" Tim went over and grabbed Bryce's shirt. Bryce tried to pull away to no avail as Cecil came toward him, refreshed and more ready to fight. Tim wouldn't let go even as his shirt started ripping, so Bryce landed a hard punch on Tim's face and broke free.

I saw the immediate danger of the situation, and knew the poor kid was in serious trouble. He'd stand no chance against the two of them together. I ran toward Eddie's truck and tried to wake him up. Eddie was a short, powerful little guy, but he'd started passing out at the start of all of the commotion. Now he finally stirred, but I knew he'd be useless in his waking drunken stupor. Tara just watched dumbly and with a beer to her lips. I don't know what she felt, but it was probably the same hopelessness I was beginning to feel. I felt a whirling stirring of the wind and my chest seemed to rise, and knew something was not well.

Tim and Cecil caught Bryce after about fifty yards when he tripped over some sagebrush. I was pissed and yelled, "Somebody fucking stop them!" at the top of my lungs. "They're beating up that kid!"

That seemed to start some action. Tara ran over to shake Eddie fully awake. Tim's other friend Keith started running to the fight and was yelling, "Hey, hey, hey! Chill out now!"

It was too late.

I got to them and something more than my worst possible fears for the kid came to be: Tim was stabbing him all over. Bryce even had stabs in his face, or at least it looked that way. His face was so covered in a thick gooey blood it bubbled out where his mouth and nose must have been—it was only something that used to resemble a handsome teenage kid. "Oh, my God! Oh, my God!" I fell to my knees and started sobbing.

"What the fuck Tim!" one of his friends yelled.

Both of his friends made a concerted effort to pull him off. Tim quickly hopped up and actually did swipe Cecil's arm. forcing them away. I'll never forget the rabid and demonic look in Tim's eyes as he scanned towards me: something else was behind his face, and it was not Tim.

Tim got back to stabbing Bryce with a dull *shick!* sound of cracking bones and penetrated flesh that poisoned the air around us over and over. I still can't ever get that sickening noise out of my head.

"Please, Tim, stop it!" I kept sobbing weakly almost as a chant to no avail.

His friends just watched dumbfounded and as powerless as I, perhaps fearing if they intervened again they'd be next.

"Holy shit!" Eddie yelled. He had a large rock in his hand, ready to smash and bash. "Tim!...Tim! What the fuck you doing?!"

That broke us all out of our trances, even Tim. He casually got up with blood all over his face as if nothing had happened, observing the one who used to be his own cousin in silence. He wiped some of the blood off his lips and spat. "Fucking punk," he said.

Eddie came over and hustled me away from the danger zone. Bryce was finished. He could only protect us from Tim's harm now.

"You better not fucking snitch!" I remember Tim

yelling as Eddie helped me into the truck.

Eddie drove us across the bumpy dirt road in silence. Sure Eddie was drunk, but we were too and I was crying with Tara holding and calming me. He seemed serious enough to drive briefly, and I know me or Tara wouldn't have driven any better. We got to Tara's house and all of us hesitated on what we'd do next.

"We got any beer?" Eddie said.

It seemed like a dubious thing to crave under those particular circumstances, but I really wanted some as my chest and throat felt closed and dry. My head hurt, too.

"Well?" I said as we both looked at Tara.

We all laughed. Tara just smiled and nodded. Of course she had some. We got out the truck and she pulled out a box of beer with about a dozen beers in it. "I stashed it at the beginning. Shit, I pitched in ten anyway. Stuck it in the truck for the hangover tomorrow."

"Lifesaver!" Eddie said.

She was. We quietly snuck into her room turned on the radio. Someone would have to eventually speak, but everyone just looked at the little speakers emitting an old Guns N Roses song on the radio, *November Rain*. I cracked a beer and threw Eddie and Tara one as well.

"Messed up, Tim—that asshole," Tara finally said after a long minute.

"What are we gonna do?" I said.

Tara and I expected Eddie to give us some answer, to be the leader. He just shook his head and said, "Nothing we can do. That kid's dead."

Without saying anything, we agreed he was right. Who wanted to be a 'snitch' and have to testify or whatever? The murder case would probably get botched, plus Tim would probably get out on self-defense or some lame manslaughter charge anyway so much was his family's influence and FBI indifference to reservation murders. Then he'd be out after a few years if he ever was convicted and come after us. We'd never even seen that Bryce kid until that night. As bad as we felt for what happened to him and as much as I wanted to cry for him again, we just sat there and stupidly drank our warm beer in solemn silence.

***

The next few days went by with all the reservation repetitiveness I'd grown bi-polarly fond of loving and hating. I wanted college to start tomorrow, to get the hell away from it all, but I still had another hot month and a half of rez drama to deal with. I mostly hung out by myself those following days. At night I walked the hills, still half-dazed from the bloody event I'd witnessed, but never daring to fully think about it. The white mounded sandstone I walked atop and along side of near the hills next to us our town would make soothing flute-like noises as the night breezes talked through and to it. I usually tried to hear what it said, but not then. I knew it was sad and angry. I visited a couple of old Indian burials set atop scaffolding from a distance a few times, but I dared not get too close to them. A person had stolen artifacts from one those graves before and sold them. Within a year two of his three sons had died.

What would our ancestors think of all of this? They'd be more than saddened. Cheyennes are banned from the tribe physically and in the afterlife for killing one of their own because they're no longer considered their true self.

I stayed up late writing, watching movies, and would sleep until the early afternoon and no one bothered me since my mom worked as a flag person for a road construction crew somewhere nearby. All I knew is that she left early in the morning and went to bed early. She was in prison from the time I was five to the time I was thirteen, and that's why I stayed at Eddie's parents after my grandma had a stroke and eventually moved into a nursing home. It was a mixture of charges my mom got sentenced for, but it came down to selling drugs. Imagine her pain when she got out and knew that her eldest and very bright son had also been busted for drugs and was serving 10 years in a federal prison. Me mess with those hard drugs? That was too harsh of a lesson learned for the both of us. It would've been five years for my brother, but he also had a hunting rifle in his house and that added on another five mandatory years. I mean, every family in Montana owns a hunting rifle. He was not using it with his alleged trafficking or whatever! Everyone knew he shot a lot of game with that gun and would personally butcher the meat for us and local elders.

Mom worked hard all the time and did every job from firefighting to road work to support me as best she could, and was going to buy me a car for getting into college and making her so proud so I could travel the 500 plus miles back and forth on breaks. I guess she was trying to make up for lost time, but we still had an odd relationship as we rarely spoke to each other. It was almost as if she was overly nice and too polite when she did speak to me. People told me she was not quite the same person she was before going to prison. I knew she felt guilty for not being there for us, and I could tell it ate her up on the inside. She was such a beautiful, good hearted person. I just wished some decent guy would marry her and treat her well so she could get on with life fully again.

My father? He'd left me when I was three and moved out of state somewhere—maybe Seattle. Someone knowledgeable told me he worked seasonal fishing jobs in Alaska. At least I got a little child support money from him and some extra, but not since I turned eighteen. That sucked. All I know about him otherwise is that he was a half-breed.

***

When they finally found Bryce's body after two days, the autopsy report said he'd been stabbed 53 times. I don't know why they include those numbers in the news brief. Must we know he was stabbed exactly 53 times? Can't they just say "stabbed multiple times"?

I felt as if I had a long hangover the whole week after Bryce kid was killed. No one came forward to testify, and everyone just kind of holed up when the FBI came around to question people. Local Bureau of Indian Affair Police were not allowed to prosecute major crimes. I'm sure Tim just plead probably plead ignorance and said he was with Sarah or something. I saw him and his buddies cruising up in a new black Ford F-150 truck about a week and a half after it happened. They pulled up to me and said they were going to go to Billings and get a motel room to party in for a week. I don't know why they felt obliged to tell me this. I politely said, "Oh, have fun."

I guess they wanted to see if I had any vibes coming off me or if I'd say anything about that incident. They must have been satisfied as they tossed me a Bud Light and sped off. I cracked open the semi-cold beer and drank it in two drinks. So good on a ninety-nine-degree day.

I walked to Tara's house and she was just baby-sitting her younger 2-year-old infant sister, Mona. The kid had been crying but stopped as soon as she saw me, her 'auntie Eva.' I embraced her tightly. I was technically Mona's cousin, but Tara and I might as well been sisters. In the 'Indian way' we were.

"So how's life? Where's your mom?" I asked her.

"I don't know. Jim Town Bar or something drinking around," she said sounding bored. The Jim Town Bar was just off the reservation border. "Maybe Lame Deer. I've been watching this kid for like two days now. I just wanna get drunk or something!"

"Really," I said. "Why is that not surprising? Hah hah! Watching the kid for two days, huh? She all right?"

"No, she keeps crying for her mom right now. Enit, Mona?"

Mona started fussing again at the mention of her

mother. "Mumma!"

"Moaning Mona! Shaw, this one," Tara said. "Her 'mumma' better get home by tonight. You got any money? I can get Uncle Joe to stop in Hardin for us. He said he'll take Mona later too if my mom ain't around still."

"No money," I said. "I didn't catch my mom this morning to ask. I should have, I was still awake. But I had one beer earlier. Fucking Tim gave it to me!"

She was pondering something. "No shit, huh? I gotta plan since my mom probably won't be back until tomorrow."

"What's that?"

"I know where my mom's stash is. Fuck it, I've been watching sis Mona here for the last two days while she's out getting drunk. I'd be surprised if she even remembers she still has that whiskey when she's back."

See, I would have stayed with my Tara's mom—or my aunt—when I was growing up, but she's never been very stable mentally and my mom knew that. My Uncle Joe was only a wild eighteen-year-old teenager at that time.

She went and retrieved the whiskey and we both made ourselves mixers with the Black Velvet and Pepsi. Mona had fallen asleep, and we watched cable TV on the couch. I wondered out loud where Eddie was.

Tara said, "He called last night and said he'd be over today. I don't know if I believe him though." A loud little pick-up pulled in the driveway. "Speak of the Devil," Tara smiled slyly and glanced out the curtain. "Who's that with him? Da-a-amn!"

I looked out the curtain and also noticed the person he'd come with. I remembered seeing him briefly a couple years ago. It was Eddie's cousin Anthony. He was from Billings—which was the largest town in Montana about one-hundred miles from Busby—and my God he was pretty. I'd actually looked up to him since I heard he was a young published writer and also Northern Cheyenne. He'd been fairly successful as a writer from what I'd heard, so I admired his brain more than I did his appearance, which seems like a brazen lie on the surface considering how naturally dazzling he looked.

We let them in. Anthony actually remembered me but seemed slightly embarrassed when Tara shook his hand and then petted his arm in jest. "Can I keep him, Eddie? Ay-y-ye!"

I'd never seen Tara act that way before, so it must have been the whiskey she was drinking. Maybe, except for the fact that we were barely buzzed. I found myself coveting her actions.

Anthony asked if it was cool if he could get his beer and bring it in. Of course he could! He came back in with a 30-pack and handed them out.

"Thank you so much, seriously," Tara said. "I was going nuts! This week is killing me."

"No problem," Anthony said. "I had to stock up in Hardin. I never really drank beers around here before, 'cept maybe in Lame Deer once. But anyway, I had to visit my patriotic American cousin here before he went into the Army."

He patted Eddie's shoulder. I'd remembered Anthony

being less talkative the last time I'd seen him, but that was right after a funeral at a feed so he'd been distant. I could tell the few beers he'd already had made him more talkative, much to me and Tara's good fortune.

For most of the afternoon we talked about weird things like how the 'kids these days' kept bringing guns to schools and shooting everyone up. We mocked and made fun of a dumb movie on T.V. for awhile, and Eddie and Anthony got sidetracked by a conversation about the whole history of war practically. Anthony was like an encyclopedia. He seemed to be very studious and you could tell it wasn't just pretend knowledge that people who just liked hearing themselves b.s. possessed. Tara and I could sit there and listen to him talk all day—if it wasn't about stupid war—and he always listened politely. He had a voice so different from anyone around the rez. He sounded almost like a white stoner dude, which sort of made sense since he was half-white himself. He was just so casual, polite, and mellow that you couldn't help but like him.

It was Anthony's idea to go into the hills later that afternoon after we dropped Mona off at our uncles. Our uncle had just come from the Wal Mart in Billings and had all kinds of goodies. Mona seemed happy to be out of the house after her nap. I know Tara was more than happy.

Since Anthony wanted to check out the 'wilderness,' we'd oblige him. However, we avoided the area of where Bryce had died and traveled on a dirt road on the opposite side of the highway.

Anthony stuck his head in the window from the back

and asked, "Did y'all know that kid that died, that dude who was like 16 or something?" We were silent. "Stabbed 53 times. Messed up, ain't it?"

"Yeah, I guess," Eddie said. We were all half busy trying to not spill our beer on the bumpy dirt road. We weren't sure if we should say anything or not, but Eddie finally spoke to his cousin. I guess he needed to confess it to someone. "We didn't know him, but we were there when it happened."

"No way, dude! Really?" Anthony said.

"Yeah," I said.

Eddie made his own road for about a quarter of a mile. He pulled over on top of a steep gully and we had a good view of the setting sun. We put the tailgate down and started sipping more beers. I had a decent buzz by then, and I presumed Tara did too. Anthony and Eddie looked normal. We discussed that bloody night and Tim.

"We couldn't do nothing...that dude just psycho'ed out," I said. "He stabbed him and kept going and going. His own friends tried to stop him and they almost got stabbed up! One did, I think."

Anthony and all of us pondered this hard. He seemed truer than anyone else I'd met in a long time. I suppose we all needed a third party to finally talk about it with since we never mentioned it to each other. The three of us being back in the country together brought back frightful memories.

Anthony said, "Happens here too much, doesn't it?"

This caught us off guard somewhat, but we knew the unfortunate answer.

"Yeah," Eddie said. "Hasn't happened for a bit, but it happens every little while. It's pretty messed up. It's always out of nothing."

"Fascinating," Anthony said. "Well, not 'fascinating.' Anyway, and I suppose no one gets caught, right?"

"They do...occasionally," Eddie said.

"Yeah, like one out of every ten times!" Tara said.

"But nothing much ever happens though unless someone takes revenge into their own hands," Eddie said. "This Bryce kid that got stabbed, no one around here even knew him—must be tough for his family back in Crow. Actually, I doubt his family even considers that his own cousin did it. Now the Crows will probably try to fight or jump every Cheyenne they see for a bit—or I hope it doesn't escalate like that, but it's human nature to want revenge. Goddamn, how can you fault their outrage? Bastard killed him, and then went to his funeral in Crow. I don't know if he's even sad or feeling guilty about it. Probably not though. Guy's a full-blown asshole."

"Crows jump me for being Cheyenne?" Anthony said. "Hmm. I know a few of 'em. Probably more of them than I do Cheyenne's, actually! They don't ever mind me. That's a result of living in Billings though: you get to know people as Indians just like you first, then what tribe they are. You can tell they're Crow by way they look of course cuz they're usually taller and lankier. We have our tribal pride and all, but like my white dude friends think it's weird to hate someone whose the 'wrong kind' of Indian. They never understood inter-tribal prejudices, and neither can I sometimes in this day and age 125 years later. But I just say it's probably like Germans and British and French people not liking each other. It's not half as bad as it used to be, I hear though. But there are good and bad in every sect of people, et cetera."

"So, what do you think of all this mess anyway?" I said. "The Tim dude?"

"What do I think?" he said. "I think that this Tim sounds pretty out of order. I don't know if I'd want to meet him. Sounds like a guy you have to kill out of self-defense before he even looked at you to protect yourself! But yeah, unless he becomes a full-fledged born again Christian in the immediate future, he's probably gonna kill again."

"You think?" I said.

"Yup," he said. "People like him, they're on a one way trip to permanent prison eventually. Just seems that way from what I conjured listening to you guys. Now that he thinks he'll get away with it—*knows* he'll get away with it...I don't know. The dad dying didn't help bring out the good side to him if he ever had one."

"Ooh, scary!" Tara said. "What do you do then? You're on the outside looking in, dude. Ah, *siva!* This one really has me saying 'dude,' enit?"

"I know, me too!" I said.

I thought about the look that Tim had on his face while shanking that poor kid, those eyes that looked as if they belonged on a bad spirit. He was not Tim.

"What do you do?" Anthony said. "What Private Eddie

said: you'd have to take matters into your own hands. We live in Montana, the place infamous and known for vigilante action. I doubt you'll commit to such a drastic measure though." He took a big shot of his beer and burped loudly. "Excuse me. I wouldn't. But...you might if the next person he kills is kin. If you did, you'd have to all be part of it —like the vigilantes. That way just one poor soul isn't the only one responsible for killing some jerk."

"You sort of make sense," Eddie said. "But I can't tell if you're just buzzed up though! What are you trying to say?"

Anthony asked for a cigarette and Tara gave him one of her last. He lit it and blew out the smoke. Smoking does not look that cool, but that was the first time I saw Anthony smoke something besides a joint, and he looked like he should have been in a flashy and sexy magazine ad for menthol cigarettes. Well, that's my exceeded opinion anyway!

"What I'm saying," he said, "is that you'll all have to put him down together eventually—preferably sooner than later. He's like a rabid dog, ya know? And you know what they have to do to rabid dogs."

"Like Cujo," I said.

"Did you know Stephen King was so 'coked out' and faded for a while there he doesn't even remember writing that 'Cujo' story?" Anthony said.

He was full of fun facts like that. God, I was so in love with him. He had a peculiar way about him that was so anti-typical yet down to Earth.

I guess it made perfect sense—his 'rabid dog theory.'

As messed up as his reasoning sounded in modern society, at the time it seemed there was no law but what we made it in the Wild West. The police stationed in Lame Deer hardly ever drove through Busby. The FBI took over hardcore cases, but what did some FBI Agent who hated being marooned on a rez in the first place care about the local populace? We never took Anthony too seriously right then, and I don't think he took himself seriously either, but we recognized he did have a valid point.

Did I ever get the guy of my dreams, Anthony? No. But I'd still marry him someday and make smart pretty Cheyenne babies, I figured. Ay-y-ye!

***

A body turned up a week later. No one knew who killed him, but based on the brutality of the crime we had a good hunch of who it was. That damned Tim, anyway. The victim was some twenty-year-old named Dwight who'd taken credit for 'finding' Bryce's body. Dwight's little kid brother and his friend had actually found the body while on a motorcycles—poor kids were traumatized—but Dwight had informed the police on where to find it.

Dwight was half-slow and everyone knew it. He was what one would call extremely naive if not 'special.' People wondered what kind of demented person could ever kill such a harmless kidlike guy as small as Dwight was. He was beaten with a blunt object that coroners figured to be a tire iron and stabbed for good measure in the heart. His whole face and head were so swollen that they had to have a closed casket funeral.

This incident sparked actual outrage throughout the community. People started asking questions, 'Did their kid know anything? Somebody did! Speak up!' Of course, no one had seen what happened. The last time Dwight was seen he was riding his bike around as usual one night. Now, no one would let their kids venture outside when it was dark.

A few days later after the FBI had come and left once again, the three of us all sat on Tara's back stoops and pondered the fucked up tragedies in our little community—feeling responsible for not having turned Tim in earlier. After the flurry of community activity that came and went like a dust devil, everything was eerily normal again. We had no full proof it was Tim that had done the crime, but that was irrelevant. It was obvious.

"We should listen to Anthony, man," Tara said.

We nodded. I pointed out that we didn't even know that Tim was around when this second murder happened. We just heard the bad news, and knew too little and too late it was Tim.

"I can shoot him," Eddie smiled to himself and held up an imaginary rifle and shot it. "Pew-w-wck! Sniper him out."

"That would be good," I said. "But I don't want you to go to prison forever just for killing *him*, just in case the FBI ever does attempt to catch someone."

"Well, what do we do?" Tara said.

"We gotta do what Anthony said. It's the only way," Eddie was serious.

"But how?" I said. "I wish he was here now."

"Of course you do, whore!" Tara teased me and playfully hit me on the arm a little too hard.

We all went through private scenarios in our head of how to murder someone and get away. My personal ideas consisted of making things look like an accident. It was way too far fetched to actually do, but fun to think of on this night. Poison his alcohol, make it look like he committed suicide with a gun, or hang him—elaborate things of that ilk that weren't very feasible.

We spotted someone large walking on the street in the distance, and as he neared we saw it was Cecil. He noticed us and came toward us. We eyed him silently until he was a few feet from us. He nodded.

"What the fuck you want?" Eddie said coldly.

I felt like seconding his words but only said, "Yeah?"

He was more than guilty by association and he knew it —picking fights with younger kids like that anyway. He should have turned Tim in, and not make us feel shitty about it. He looked scared and worried, though unfazed by our rudeness.

"I don't know what to do, man. He's lost it," he said.

"What are you talking about?" Eddie said.

"Tim," he said. I saw his eyes start to swell up with tears somewhat. I actually felt bad for the oaf. "He's lost it! I just came from his house, and he beat the fuck out of Sarah. She didn't even do nothing! He just said she 'snitched' on him to the feds."

"So he's been drinking a lot?" I said.

"Yeah," he said. "Not just that though. He's been slamming shit—crystal."

That complicated matters just a little more, as well as simplify things. He meant he was using methamphetamine, a plague in Montana that certainly hadn't neglected rural areas like ours. 'Slamming' meant he used a syringe to inject the drug. "How long has he been shooting up?" Eddie said.

"He's been doing it the last few months since his dad died, but he's been shooting up 'bout the last month and a half. He's lost it."

"So we know," Eddie said. "Why'd you come talk to us about it?"

"I've been wanting to talk to you guys...since that night. You guys were the only one's there besides us guys. You saw how bad he's gotten. You're the only one's that'll believe me. In Billings he almost killed me. We had to wrestle him down, and then he blamed me for us guys getting kicked out of that motel." A tear rolled down his cheek. "I'm scared, man," he choked. "I just don't know what to do about that guy anymore!"

I asked about Keith.

"He's watching Tim right now, making sure he don't track Sarah down," Cecil said. "He don't care any more what happens to Tim. He wants to take him out himself and go to prison for it. Sarah is his best cousin, you know?"

"Yeah, we know," Eddie said. "We know. I tell you what, you get Keith tomorrow to meet us here at nine in the morning if you want our help. You guys think you can wake up by then?"

"I was gonna go crash for a bit, but yeah," Cecil said. "Keith's just sort of baby sitting Tim. Tim's was already crashing out, but I'll make sure Keith don't kill him in his sleep or do something ignorant he'll get busted for. I don't think Keith will sleep tonight, if you know what I mean."

He meant that Keith was also high on meth. Eddie nodded and just told him to remember: 9 o'clock a.m., same spot.

***

Ten hours later we talked and devised our plan. There were a few isolated heavy clouds out. It was sprinkling lightly, but it wasn't going to rain hard anytime soon. I could oddly see the sun shining and blue sky all around us otherwise. Wait 15 minutes if you don't like the weather in Montana.

There was me, Tara, Eddie, Cecil, and Keith. Our plan was simple: we'd all get together with Tim in a remote party spot in the country, and kill him with his own knife that he kept under his truck seat, just like he did to his victims.

We had to do it. Otherwise, one of us or another innocent person might be next. Screw the cops and feds.

So it was final, and Eddie had finalized the plan and Tim's appreciative friends would make sure Tim came.

"Then it's settled," Eddie said. "Don't tell anyone where you're going today. No one. If anyone has the slightest whim of where you are or where you're going, it's canceled. Keep a low profile all day. Hole up in a room and smoke fucking meth all day for all I care. Clear?" Eddie shook each one of our hands and asked while looking into our eyes if we were cool. "I'll go to Hardin and get some beer to lure him with. Who wants to come?"

"Not me," Tara yawned. "I'm going back to sleep."

The boys shook their heads no.

"I'll go," I said, even though I was as tired as Tara. I couldn't possibly sleep at a time like this, I thought. "I need to take a cruise."

Hardin was some cool little hick town next to the Crow Indian Reservation that adjoined our rez about 40 miles from Busby. On the way there and back you'd drive right next to the Little Big Horn Battlefield on the Crow rez. I remember seeing pictures from back in perhaps the 1940's that showed the signs of the bars in Hardin that said, 'No Dogs or Indians Allowed.' It was messed up, but it was still also funny to me for some reason. Fucking humans. I fell asleep on the ride there, contrary to my earlier thoughts about 'not being able to possibly sleep.' The warm air from the fresh sunlight and soothing movement of the car made me forget all of the drama going on. We wouldn't kill Tim, I thought in my doze as my mind drifted away. No reprisal would be necessary, because it was all just a passing nightmare, and Tim had never murdered anyone. I slept soundly.

"Hey!" Eddie woke me up as he stepped out of his truck. "Put fifteen dollars of gas in, would ya please? I know this bro here. He'll let me buy. Won't even have to find some wino."

I knew the plan was unfolding and my dream of peace

was only a dream. I watched the gas pump numbers tick up. Eddie was inside talking and laughing with some store clerk white guy buddy. Everything was in slow motion. I didn't know where he knew the clerk from, which was amazing since I thought I knew everyone Eddie knew—even if they didn't know me.

He came out with two eighteen packs, a twelve pack, and four 24 ounce cans for our personal enjoyment.

"Lotta beer this early in the morning, Ed," I said.

"I know!" He was extremely hyper and jovial. "My mom won in Bingo, and I borrowed like fifty bucks from her. It's all for the cause though. Gimme one of those anyway."

Ah yes, 'the cause.' The cause of luring and murdering a fellow teen. But Tim was not innocent. That I had to remember. I handed Eddie a beer and cracked one open myself.

"Little early to be drinking this early in the morning, Eva! Ay-y-ye!" Eddie sarcastically said with a laugh.

I could not fathom how he could be in such fine spirits, but when Led Zeppelin's "Kashmir" song came on the radio, I also forgot the devious task ahead and drifted into a mellow euphoria as we shared a cigarette. The Little Bighorn Battlefield hill and monument where 'Custer last stood' loomed in the short distance. I had missed it on the way in when I slept. Though I passed by it hundreds of times, I still smiled—a little sadistically—every time I saw Custer's headstone with all of the other soldiers' grave markers scattered about it. It gave me a warm feeling to know that what went around came around to Custer and his unfortunate five companies of men at that celebrated spot in 1876 as he attacked the Cheyenne side of the Indian allied camp. It was the Native Americans' gift for the United States' Centennial birthday.

***

Nothing really happened for the rest of that on and off cloudy Wednesday afternoon. I chilled out in Eddie's room on a comfortable armchair and tried to forget about everything. It was sad; that poor Bryce kid, and our friendly neighborhood Dwight with their entire lives ahead of them, both brutally killed. We'd no longer see Dwight cruising his cheap mountain bike around he was so proud of and always kept shiny. I tried not to think of these things, but their faces kept creeping into my brain, haunting me.

I thought of the dream I had of Dwight and Bryce the previous night. I dreamed they came to see me in my room, bloody and beaten, and they asked why I didn't help them.

"I'm sorry!" is all I could tell them. "I tried. I tried. I did all I could. Please, understand!"

But this was not true and the ghosts let me know this as they shook their heads in disapproval. I could have tried to break up the fight between Bryce and Cecil myself, and they would have perhaps stopped. I could have told the police something about Tim to at least prevent Dwight's death, but I never did. This they let me know silently: that I was guilty for by standing by when something could have been averted.

"I'm sorry!" is all I could say again. I really meant the

words, but words were no good to them. "What can I do, please?"

"It's not over," they said.

It was disturbing all right, but when I woke up it seemed to make me more determined than scared. I wondered if anyone else had a similar dream. Perhaps they were real ghosts and not a dream. I recalled a story about various people seeing a couple of ghost girls in their car while they were driving to Lame Deer. The girls were best friends, and they'd supposedly died in a car wreck on that same road back in the 1970's. They are said to haunt people by mysteriously appearing without warning in people's back seat at night from time to time, just smoking cigarettes and laughing away—perhaps doing the last thing they'd ever done. I didn't want Bryce or Dwight ever haunting me. I knew we had to finish it whether it was a dream or ghosts.

Eddie went about his usual work out routine with his push-ups, sit-ups, whatever—just getting ready for his Army basic training all day. I couldn't tell what was going through his mind, but I had a feeling he was just anxious to get it all over with. The sooner the better. He went on one of his long jogs, and I called Anthony's cell phone.

"Hello?"

"This is Evalyn, remember me?"

"Oh yeah! What's up Eva? You're the one that's going to be the writer! Cool."

"Yeah. I just needed someone to talk to. Are you busy?"

"No, not really. Just finished some class up at the college here. I'm just sitting on the grass, actually. But not on grass! Waste of time anyway."

"What's a waste of time, college?"

"No, just joking! But I don't know. I just don't think college is right for me. The only reason I come is...well...this is where all the chicks are."

"You're so weird!"

I felt so comfortable talking to him even though I'd never met anyone remotely like him. I sensed that he was a loner much like myself. He'd already told me before he hardly personally knew anyone and no one knew him aside from his byline.

"So I heard about that dude who got killed...again."

"Yeah, messed up," I said. "You were right."

"Unfortunately. You guys gonna...you know?"

"Yes."

"'Nuff said. So that's what's bothering you?"

"Yeah, but I wanted to ask you something; about college."

I settled back into the armchair and asked him what it was like. He said it was all right—way better than high school —but he didn't feel he had any uses for it. He knew it sounded pretentious, but he just didn't even have any idea of what to even start majoring in. He just wanted to write, work whatever jobs, and send out stuff to publishers. He said classes 'dulled his mind.' I couldn't tell if he was joking as he did speak fluent sarcasm a lot.

He obviously knew of my goals of wanting to be a writer. We'd talked at length about that. I wanted advice on what I should major in at the university aside from general studies and English classes.

"You're asking me?" he said. "Funny. But you're going to the University of Montana, and you want to be a writer. Hmm...besides from creative writing, I'd just do journalism, I guess. They have one of the best schools for that. A top 10 in the country school. Plus, you'd get paid to write for a full-time job. That's what I'd do."

"That sounds pretty good. Someone mentioned that before, but I never thought too much about it. Why don't you do journalism if 'that's what you'd do'?"

"I'd hate having to write newspaper writing and inhibit my pen from doing magical wonders."

I laughed. "But you want *me* to do it?"

"Well, I was being facetious. I do it, but I don't know, dude. An English Degree doesn't do me any good though, since I wouldn't ever want to teach. Journalism...I wouldn't hurt getting my degree in it and being official. I'm actually considering it now! It's like a light bulb went off."

"But you've already published a lot of articles. How did that happen?"

"Eh, I lied on my query letters and told them I had an advanced degree from Colombia University and they'd have to accept my work—even if it was garbage—or be deemed an unworthy publication. Hah hah! Kidding. I studied markets, wrote what I thought was interesting within that market, asked questions to knowledgeable people, and yadda, yadda, yadda!"

"So you don't need school?"

"Of course I need school, but I just find no use for English classes and whatnot. I just do art here. I couldn't tell you anything about adjectives and predicates or whatever. I loathe that stuff. But I do read like four or more hours everyday. That's my English and history class combined into one. I read a ton of history. I actually just got out of history class, too."

"'Four or more hours'? Damn."

"Yeah, now I can be lazy and call it 'studying.' Hah! Or more sadly I'm just a reclusive geek. But don't think for two seconds about not going to school. I have faith in you. You're a smart girl and kids around you need someone to look up to."

"What about you?"

"Kids look up to me? God, I hope not."

"Not that!"

We talked for a while longer and I tried to convince him he should transfer to the school I was going to. He said he'd think about it, but loved Billings. At least I solidified what seemed like an already good friendship that day. Also, he said he'd help me with writing advice anytime.

His words helped the rest of that decisive afternoon drift by more easily as I kept replaying what he'd said.

***

The clouds grew denser on the overcast horizon at dusk.

I couldn't help but think how much I'd miss squeezing into Eddie's little orange truck with Tara once the summer was over with. I'd be off to college and Eddie would be gone too. We drifted over the dirt road bumping and rolling along with Tim driving his new F-150 Ford truck behind us. My God, it was actually going to happen. This was premeditated murder, but only we knew that. Of course if anyone suspected any of us and one of us actually got caught, we'd bind together as witnesses and say it was self-defense from the dreaded psychopath Tim. In addition, the truth about Tim killing those other two people would come to light. Our plan was way tight.

I glanced behind us in the rear view mirror and saw Tim laughing and joking. Keith seemed to have a knowing grin on his face, and Cecil looked worried.

We finally stopped the trucks, and I couldn't help but notice we were about quarter mile from where Anthony had given us the idea to 'off' Tim. Eddie must have planned it that way. Eddie made a surprisingly efficient killer. Maybe the Army was the best place for him.

We had our two full 18 packs, and a few beers leftover from the twelve pack Eddie and I had started on that morning and early afternoon. I'd taken a power nap earlier on Eddie's armchair, but I was burnt out otherwise. Another beer would help rejuvenate me for the long night ahead.

"Hey! We should throw some of those in here!" Tim said as he proudly pulled out a little cooler.

"Nice," Eddie said as he signaled to me to do just that. Cheyenne women are always expected to work!

Off the Path

We all sat quite and stared off into the steep rolling hills for awhile, just sipping away. Well, everyone except Tara. She burped and was grabbing another beer before anyone else had but three drinks. She'd been even more quite than usual that day, and started organizing the little cooler so the maximum amount of beer and ice could fit in there. We all watched her for a second before we lost interest. Well, except for the boys casually staring at her ass 'enjoying the scenery,' as they say to each other. There were some deer across the coulee, but they paid no heed to us.

It was naturally a bit uncomfortable, this tailgate party of ours, but after a few beers people started talking. Tim thanked Eddie for the beer, and Tara pulled out most of a bottle of the Black Velvet whiskey we'd been drinking the day Anthony showed up. I had forgotten that we'd never drank it up, and I was surprised that Tara had never did by then either. She wasn't much of a whiskey drinker, however.

We passed the bottle around, and someone, I think it was Cecil, said they wished they had some grass.

I remembered that I'd stashed Anthony's roaches in Eddie's truck after we'd smoked that night. I retrieved them and everyone was happy as we puffed them out of a makeshift beer can pipe.

The high slowly went away along with the rest of the daylight. Dark out; all of us satisfied with our buzzes, all of us calm.

We all had sweatshirts or jackets on due to the day's cloudiness. I saw a thick spark of lightning through the clouds off in the distance.

Tim started to speak as if the rumbling thunder that followed cued him.

"You know, for about two weeks after my dad died, I put a rifle to my head every night," he said slowly. "I wanted to kill myself so fucking bad. I don't even know why. I loved my dad, but I didn't even like him—if that makes sense."

"It does," Keith said. "I know how he treated you, when you'd run us guy's house at night after he'd beat y'all."

Tim looked up at us to see if we were paying attention, and we were rapt as he exposed a side to himself that we'd never deemed possible. I guess everyone feels—even Tim. He continued:

"Yup. I always had the newest shoes, toys, and video games or whatever, but it seems like it came with a heavy price. He'd beat me and my mom every few nights at least. I never even cried at his funeral. Is that bad?"

"Grief is...grief doesn't have any set rules," I said. I wanted to comfort him, but I couldn't find the right words. I don't think he was trying to get people to feel sorry for him, I don't think he knew how to do that. He was just telling the truth.

He nodded once to me and continued.

"I never wanted to be like him," his eyes glossed over a bit. "Last night...I beat Sarah—and God I love her so much— and I knew I'd turned into my dad. He beat my mom like that. I never wanted to be that. I'm sorry Keith, everyone. You guys know what I did before, too."

Keith rubbed his shoulder, "It's okay bro, we all make mistakes. I'm sorry, too."

And suddenly it finally happened. Keith had thrust the knife up and under Tim's ribs and he fell to the ground, gasping for air.

Though it was nearly black out, the flashes of lightning that had become more frequent captured the look of pain and shock on Tim's face like a camera's flash.

Tim was trying to say something as he lay on his side out of breath, but Keith handed the knife to Cecil and he stabbed him near his chest and right shoulder area. On his back, moaning, cursing, and gasping, Tim tried to get into some sort of fetal position. It was Eddie's turn, and he quickly shoved the knife below his ribs twice, handed the knife to Tara, and walked away. Tim looked pretty much out of it and finished as Tara knelt beside him and grabbed the knife handle with both hands. She cruelly plunged it into Tim's stomach, and for the first time Tim let out a horrific wail. I guess he was not all the way dead.

It was my turn, and I knelt by Tim like Tara. The high quality bone-handle hunting knife had a deadly six-inch blade. It was the same instrument that had caused so much sorrow to mothers, families, and friends over the last few weeks. I got close to Tim and I could tell he was trying to say something. I heard someone throwing up somewhere. I think it was Cecil. I listened to what Tim was trying to say.

"I'm sorry...momma," I could barely hear him. I lip read it more than I heard it. A little creek of blood started coming out of his mouth and his eyes became dull. He must have been completely dead right then—or so I tell myself every day.

"Forgive me," I said and plunged the knife directly into his chest, and left it. A stream of blood shot directly into my eye that threatened to make me puke, but I put my hands on Tim and prayed for him.

Tara put her hands on my shoulder as I cried and prayed.

"Please, Lord, forgive us. Jesus, forgive Tim. Forgive us!"

I said that simple prayer over and over. Keith started singing a song I'd heard at funerals, the Cheyenne Death Song. When translated it said:

Nothing lives long, except the Earth and the mountains

During the song I imagined the other two young people who'd been forced to go into the afterlife before their time that summer. It relaxed us all, a good song to pass into the afterlife with. 'If the word of a Cheyenne is no good, then I would rather die than live,' a warrior once said long ago. Tim was dead by the hands of those he trusted, for killing those that trusted him.

The song came to a finish, and a bolt of lighting shattered the air too close for our comfort.

Eddie helped me up. "Come on, it's finished. It's over."

Cecil regained his composure and quickly started wiping everything down to get rid of fingerprints. Keith and

Tara helped gather the beer cans in the back of Tim's truck and put them in Eddie's.

"What about that knife?" Cecil said, ready to pull it out of his former friend's chest.

"Leave it," Eddie said. "At least now they'll have a murder weapon from the last two murders. We can send an anonymous tip about the other two so they close this case quickly and not bug you guy's too much."

"Right."

Cecil wiped the knife handle well with a bandana and hopped in the back of the beat up little Datsun with Keith.

We drove out of the area casually, all of us silent. We reached the highway and with no lights on, we waited for a few cars to pass. No one saw us as we pulled onto the highway. A few miles later we were back in Busby as the first drops of rain came down.

We dropped Keith and Cecil off and gave them a few beers each to calm their nerves. Eddie gave them each a good hug and told them something I couldn't hear.

It started raining even harder as soon as we got to Tara's. We stood in the downpour outside for a bit at the back of Tara's house as if we were showering in it to get the blood and sin off of us.

Tara thought that maybe God was crying for us, for our people that mourned. Maybe he was. Eddie was more practical; he said that it was a lucky break because the rain would erase the evidence and tire tracks so we wouldn't have to move Tim's body elsewhere.

It rained all day the next day, too. Some tribes say it rains to erase all the footprints and tracks of those who had died, and where they'd been. If that was true, there were a lot of footprints to erase from those few hectic weeks. While killing someone didn't make us 'more of a man' and especially not a better human being, we all grew up that night.

I always wonder how much Eddie and Tara reflect on that night. I know Tara does a lot since I visit her at home whenever I can on holidays and breaks. She's been to alcohol treatment since, and has finally started turning her life around after an attempted suicide. She got her GED, and will be attending classes at the college in Billings. I still call her a lot too, since I felt like I abandoned her after that summer. I encourage her to stick with school—I'm in my third year of college. She slipped up in her alcohol addiction and relapsed, but at least she has direction now.

Last I heard from Eddie, he was fresh out of Army Airborne Ranger School, heading for combat somewhere. He tells me to stop beating myself up over what happened; that we did the right thing. "Some people just need to die," he tells me.

Maybe he's right.

Cecil is not doing so well though. Tara said she saw him drinking around like a wino in Billings and had just gotten out of jail after a spell. I guess he looked rough but halfway healthy at least. He was happy to see Tara though, and she gave him a few bucks. He told her to tell me that he sends his regards, so there you have it.

Off the Path

Keith has started singing in a drum group, and has been driving machines on road construction crews after living in Oklahoma for about a year. He's been mostly sober with a new family and he's doing well. No one's really talked to him about what happened that night, but I suppose he wants it that way.

And then there's Anthony, the inadvertent mastermind of it all. He's got a book coming out, and continues to talk to me through e-mails. He says I'm already a great article writer and if I keep at it I'll make a good living someday at a major publication because of it. That would be the day!

When I started off writing this story, I didn't know what I hoped to accomplish. I guess it was just a story that needed to be told—needed to be let out of my blood. However, I see no reason to 'pretty it up' by excluding the alcohol and drug references or violence to make myself or anyone else seem noble. It is how it was, and there's nothing glorifying about it.

I hope this finally puts my restless mind at ease. I hope the ghosts will let me as well as themselves rest now. Most of all, I want people to know that this story did happen, and lives on some little reservation town where General George Armstrong Custer last slept are forever different—for better or worse—because of it.

My Brother's Keeper (a novella excerpt)

By Eric Leland Bigman Brien

"And the Lord said unto Cain, where is Abel thy brother? And he said, I know not: Am I my brother's keeper."
Genesis 4:9

I have insecurities. Not the petty, little, financial insecurities or penis insecurities that young men have when they enter puberty. I don't worry if that pretty young gal in the red dress thinks I'm a handsome man. I don't question my ability to perform my custodial duties at the University of Montana in Missoula where I work. I have a great deal of insecurity pertaining to my legacy.

Legacy is something for the rich—or the brave. I push a fucking mop. I have no wealth to leave my loved ones. I have no bead work, paintings, or notebooks. As much as I don't like it, my legacy will be one of regret, unfulfilled potential, and questions. Everybody has questions. All the time, every day, questions. There are big questions, little questions, inappropriate questions, and unasked questions.

What shall I eat? What shall I wear? Where did I put my wallet? Did I pay that bill? We even ask ourselves the big questions. What is my purpose? Is there a God? What have I done with my life? I'm no different. The older I get the more questions I have. It's used to be discouraging but now it's just old and common—like me.

And right now I have only one nagging question: *who the fuck is calling me this damn early?*

I am a widower and I have never remarried. In fact, I've been a widower longer than I was married. I have a son who spends most of his time drunk; or in jail when his wife decides that she needs a break from him. They have a daughter, Lillian. She's four-years-old but already more intelligent than her parents. If my son is not calling me from jail, then it must be a wrong number.

I have been following a debt reduction plan from this guy on A.M. radio. You call in and ask him about stocks, bonds, A.P.R.'s and all those financial type of inquiries. My debts are all paid so I know it's obviously not a bill collector. It's kind of sad, I know, that I really don't have anyone to call me. I mean, the Jehovah's Witnesses won't even call me anymore because they're tired of my inquiries about the deeper meaning of why religions were invented and the like. Whoever it is will just call back. This mystery caller is indeed very persistent. This has got to be at least the third time they've called me in the last ten minutes.

"Hello, this is Jonah," I said tiredly, anticipating that I would hear the thick accent of some poor overworked bastard in India.

"Hey, it's about time you answered." No Indian accent —at least not Eastern Indian.

I knew I wasn't going to be asked to purchase some

unsolicited insurance plan or to participate in another bullshit survey for a 20 dollar gift card that would arrive in the mail in six to nine weeks. I knew this voice and I thought I'd pushed it out of my memory. After 30 years I still recognized my brother Solomon's incredibly thick and unnecessary Crow accent.

What I mean by 'unnecessary' is that our mother never actually spoke the Crow language, and our white father was unknown to us. Our mother was a product of the early reservation period, where speaking one's own language first heard across this U.S. land was essentially regarded as virtual treason in boarding schools. My brother in English, however, still always sounded like he was teaching the oral traditions around a campfire for tourists; and it always seemed more well-rehearsed and got even stoically deeper when he thought he was saying something especially profound.

I glanced over at the alarm clock that I have set to talk radio. There is this crazy conservative guy that comes on at 10 and I usually catch him about halfway through his concluding rant when I come home. Then at midnight this paranormal guy comes on and all these nut-jobs call in. I usually fall asleep listening to that. Right now some guy is bitching about the immigration problem. Tell a Native American about that one.

"Wha-a-a? It's six ten in the morning," I said realizing he probably knew it was six ten in the morning and most likely didn't care.

"No, shit. That's what time we get up in the real world.

I already got my coffee and weather." As long as I could remember he had this sarcastic little snicker when he said something he thought was witty or clever and it was always annoying, now more so than ever.

"Well I'm really fucking happy that you got your morning perk but I haven't, so say what you gotta say and let me sleep." I didn't mean to sound like such an ass. For all I knew someone could have died or something. I haven't spoken to my brother for over thirty years. It was strange because I missed him and actually wanted to talk to him sometimes, but I'd much rather hate him in silence the rest of my life.

"What? No, how have you been? How are your kids?" I could kind of hear the sting in his voice. That was something new.

"Hey, Solomon! I'm sorry. How are you? How are your kids? What the fuck you want?" I was able to leave out my own little snicker. My sarcasm was always a bit more venomous.

I could feel old feelings rise up in me. I was totally justified to feel this way. My anger was righteous. I waited for him to say something, but there was only silence. Awkward, empty silence, and then...

"I'm going to die and I want you to take care of me." He went straight to the point. I could hear the pain and restraint in his voice.

I glance at my clock radio again. 6:12 a.m., and this was already one of the longest conversations I've ever had. It still had not fully sunk in I was talking to my Son of a Bitch brother Solomon, and he was telling me that he was dying.

"You're dying? Dying from what?" I didn't know what else to say. Part of me didn't know if he was telling the truth. I think I even sounded accusatory.

"That doesn't matter." He paused and took in a deep breath. "All that matters is I don't have very long."

I finally realized that he was being serious. My thoughts immediately went back to our childhood home on the Crow Indian reservation in south eastern Montana. As small children we were always together fishing the Little Big Horn. When I turned 12 our mother gave me a new tackle box with fancy lures that I knew nothing about. I also was giving the same tan color of fancy fishing hat the fly-fishing white tourists had up in Fort Smith.

We didn't have transportation, so we didn't get to fish in Wyola or hunt in the Big Horn mountains like our cousins did. Our mother was a very strict Baptist woman so we didn't get to do much. She cleaned house and sold bead work for a living so we were very poor. We weren't poor like some local families, but compared to the real world—outside of the reservation—we were desperately and hopelessly impoverished. Statistics have proven so.

"I'm sorry to hear that brother. Really sorry," I said. I didn't know what to say to him as our younger memories still came back.

"Well, you don't need to be. I've made peace with God and my family."

I often wondered what people meant when they said that. As if making peace with God can undo everything. I wondered if my brother thought he'd 'made peace' with me and thought about asking him, but then I thought against it. I couldn't say anything. I just waited.

"Well, what do you think about it?" he asked me like it was some small favor with no weight to it whatsoever.

"I think you're fucking crazy!" There was no hiding the contempt that suddenly flooded me. "You call me up and tell me you're gonna die. You ask me to move back over there and what, quit my job? What the fuck is wrong with you? You got kids. Ask one of them."

I knew I was raising my voice at an extreme level. But one of his tactics was he'd make unreasonable requests, and then play dumb when you denied him.

"I'm not asking you to move back over here." I could hear him sigh. "I was actually thinking I could come up there and stay with you until...you know...." I could not believe what I was hearing.

"You know what? Die. You wanna come and live with me until you're dead? You wanna die in *my* house?" I wasn't just asking rhetorical questions. This was so ludicrous I had to ask to make sure that I was hearing him right. "Well, is that it?"

"Yes, that's it, and no, that's not it." He would typically answer questions like this. I never understood him.

"Yes and no? How fucking vague can you be?" I felt like ending the conversation, my forefinger hovered above the hang up button.

"Yes, I want to live with you for a short time; and yes, I plan on dying there." I sensed that he was getting nervous. He took a deep breath. "This is very difficult for me."

"Well, just say it. You've never had a problem speaking you're mind." I wasn't sure if I was following him. I always knew there was something else.

"I want to come up tomorrow, and hopefully I can make it till Easter." He said it very quickly, as if speed made his words more palatable. It took me a second before I connected the pieces.

"Hold up. Tomorrow is Ash Wednesday. So what, you wanna come for Lent?"

"Yeah." He said it like I had caught him with his hands in the cookie jar. I could picture him lowering his head like a child.

"So...you come for Lent, we go to Easter service, and we're reconciled? Then you slowly rot away on my couch? What about Sharon and the kids? What do they think of all this?"

"You need to understand how difficult this is. You know, Sharon left me over this." I'd heard his wife left him, but I didn't know why and just figured it served him right. I thought he must have gotten caught in a dog knot with one of his students or coworkers because he'd also resigned his teaching position at the university in Billings. "She didn't have the stomach for this, and I didn't have the stomach to ask the kids this."

"What? She didn't have the stomach to take care of her sick husband? I don't believe it." I couldn't see how Sharon could be so cold to him after all these years.

"No, I'm sure she'd take wonderful care of me. No one could do better. And yes, she doesn't have the stomach to help me die."

My brain froze. Of course, he wanted her to kill him! Now that she wouldn't do it, he wanted me to. It took me awhile to gain what little composure that a nude, old man with morning breath could as I shook the rest of the cobwebs from my brain. To me the answer was obvious. All this waiting to die was too much for him and he was losing his mind.

"As much as I've wanted to see you dead in the last thirty years, and as much as you deserve it, I'm not going to kill you. I think that you need help, and I don't think that you should call me anymore."

I hung up the phone as he tried to say something, my thoughts conflicting as I did.

Conflict has to be the word that describes mankind best. Without conflict there is no story, no outcome, and no lesson. If conflict describes mankind then warfare best describes the Crow people. Warfare is conflict in action. Every Crow knows this from the ones counting coup in foreign wars to the ones trying to put down the bottle. It is bred deeply into our spirits and flesh. Warfare is constant to the Crow. If I defeat my enemy, then what do I do? There is much conflict in me.

My thoughts went back to Solomon and our

childhood. I thought about my wife Lilly and how much I missed her. I thought about the pain that I'd put her and our son through. Mostly I thought about how things would have been if I had never caught Solomon with Lilly.

Suddenly the phone rang again, pulling me out of thoughts. I wiped the tears away from my eyes, and cleared my throat. This would be the last time he made me cry. I was going to tell him how I felt. I was going to tell him to rot in hell. I was breathing heavily. I picked up the phone.

"Listen up!" I said, but it wasn't Solomon.

"This is the Yellowstone County Detention Center. Would you like to accept a collect phone call from–"

"Fuck!" I knew this wasn't good. This was already a long day of questions, and it was just starting.

Bloody Hands

By Cinnamon Spear

With summer around the corner, my mom thought it best to put my sister on birth control as a precautionary measure because she noticed the closeness growing between her and Samson. After triage and my sister peeing in a cup for the required pregnancy test, the two sat while a lack of words filled the space between them in the exam room. Lord knows what thoughts tumbled through their heads until the nurse returned with the wrong three-syllable word.

"Are you ready to be a mom now, Faith? You don't even know how to respect your own mother!" she snarled as a footrace towards the exit ensued.

"Shut up. Just don't talk to me!"

"Don't talk to you? Don't talk to you? You're going to need me more than ever! How do you think you and your baby are going to get along in life without me? Your better be ready to face your dad."

"Just shut up!"

Two automatic doors slid in opposite directions and my mother and sister did the same. Mom took a sharp left and started walking towards the house, which is a half-mile north of the clinic, and my sister headed towards town, ready to take on the world alone. Dad returned home from running errands and mother greeted him.

"Your daughter's pregnant."

"What? You're kidding me!"

"Eight weeks."

"Where is she?"

"She started walking up town, telling me to shut up like she knows it all."

"God dammit, Marie! You let her walk into town alone? She has nowhere to go! Get in the car and don't say a word. You're not allowed to talk to her."

"Oh I don't *need* to talk to her, she's thinks she knows everyth—"

"Just shut up!"

"Jesus Christ she *is* your daughter."

"Let's go."

After a short fruitful search, they were again under the same roof but the absence of acknowledgment screamed down the hallways. The bedroom, kitchen, and living room transformed into silos that held the good, the bad, and the ugly. Mom couldn't talk to Faith. Dad never even said the word *Kotex* nonetheless much more than that. Faith couldn't face either of them. Three disconnected entities in their own atmospheres, yet all orbiting the same reality. Mom's only option was to call for back up, the intermediary, the thread that brought contradictory pieces of mismatched fabric together—not to connect them, but to align them—in this quilt we call family. My phone rang.

"Hello?"

"Hey."

"Oh, hi Mom!"

"Hey. We got some news over here...your sister's pregnant."

"What the *fuck*? Are you serious?"

"Yep. Your dad threatened to kick me out again if I say anything to her. He's in there watching *Ghost Hunters* like he has no care in the world. She's locked herself in her room."

"Damn, you're serious. Does Samson know?"

"She hasn't told him yet. *We* haven't even talked about it! You need to call and talk to her. I'm not *allowed* to and she's sure and the hell not going to talk to your dad about it. I really snapped at her and I'm sure she's scared. Call back in a while and talk to her, would ya? I gotta go. I'm making lunch for your dad. He needs to take his diabetic medicine before he blows his top."

"Kay, yeah. Yeah, I will."

"Okay. I'll talk to you later. I gotta go."

"Bye."

I replaced the black handset on the receiver and sat at my school-issued, unfamiliar freshman desk. In a paralytic daze, I targeted an empty stare at some obscure gray mark on the crème colored wall. *I don't even know what sex feels like and my little sister is pregnant? Pregnant! As in she's had sex and is* pregnant. *Penis-in-my-little-sister pregnant.* The news from 2,000 plus miles away immediately weighted me with a hundred and one questions. *When was her first time? When will be my first time? Why didn't she tell me—I thought she told me everything? What does sex feel like? Wait, she's three years younger than me. She's 15, so he's only 14! They had SEX? I don't even know what sex is! What are they going to do? What are we going to do?*

After an hour of failed attempts at reading *The Woman Warrior* by Maxine Hong Kingston, the assigned reading for my Intro to Writing course, I couldn't help my curious subconscious from dragging me back to sexually explicit thoughts that included my little sister. I remembered when I was a freshman in high school and an eighth grader had a baby; she was shunned socially. I worried for my sister, but that was five years ago. Girls seem to be having babies younger and younger these days. I figured an hour was a good enough amount of time for the dust to be settled in the house. I took a deep breath.

"Hello?"

"Hey-y-y, Sis. Mom told me what's going on. You okay? I'm sure you're thinking a million things right now."

"Yeah."

"I want you to know, first of all, that I'm your big sister and I'll support you in whatever it is you choose to do. If you're ready to have this baby, I will do everything I can to help provide for diapers and everything else. I'm going to be out here for the next four years but I can try my best to help, financially. If you decide that you're not ready, well then, I'll support you as best I can that way, too. I just want you to really think about this, okay? How ya' feelin'?"

"I can't believe there's something *inside* of me right now. It's disgusting. I want it out."

My heart sank. *That something inside of you is your baby, my niece or nephew.*

"Have you thought about Samson?"

"I'm not telling him. He's the only one of his brothers that doesn't have a baby yet. I know he'll want it. I don't want it. It's *in* me right now. It's grossing me out."

"Well, what are you going to do with your life? Because if you're still gonna be with him, like if you see yourself having a family with him in the future, there's no sense in killing your first child together. This is a huge decision. You really need to think it through. I know you're a smart girl. You could attend a great college and have an awesome career; you know that? But you can't do it with a baby. I mean, you *could,* it'd just be a million times harder and it's a hundred times less likely that you would. I have confidence in you but you have to *want it.* I'm not going to encourage you either way, but I'll support you in whatever it is you choose to do."

"I know. I want to go to college and do something with my life. I want to get out of this hellhole. I don't want to be in Montana forever. I don't even want to be with him. I don't. I don't love him. I don't even *like* him..."

My head skipped like a scratched CD on "I can't believe there's something *inside* of me right now." *How could she possibly be a good mother if her own inhabited womb disgusts her? Can't babies hear everything the mom is thinking? Poor baby.* I encouraged her to think about it in isolation for a few more hours and when she felt ready, talk with Mom and Dad, as a family about it—despite how hesitant she might be to do so. Faith knew she was going to need them so she swallowed the lump in her throat and opened the door of her room, and conversation. Two entire days stretched thin before Mom rang my phone again.

"She decided she wants an abortion and we agree that it's the best thing for her. I've called the Planned Parenthood in Billings and scheduled an appointment. They said we're lucky to have caught it in the first trimester. Taking her up tomorrow but the procedure is going to cost $947. We're still waiting for your dad's back-payment check from unemployment, but even if he got it tomorrow, it wouldn't be enough."

"So what does that mean?"

"So-o-o that means we need your help. The decision's been made and the more time that passes the harder it is on everybody. Can you Western Union us $950 by the end of today?"

"It doesn't sound like I have much of a choice."

"She's been accepted to that summer program she applied for! She can use her stipends to pay you back."

"But I haven't even bought my plane ticket to come home yet."

"Your dad will help, too. You know that."

"Yeah...but..." I say dejectedly, "Can I talk to her real quick?"

"Yeah, hold on. *Fa-a-aith! Your sister's on the phone!*"

....

"Hello?"

"Hey-y-y, Sis. So you guys've talked about it?"

"Yeah. For *days*."

"And you're sure this is what you want?"

"I already told you."

"I know. I'm just making sure."

"Well I'm sure. And I'm tired of talking."

"*Okay*, well tell Mom I'll head to the bank now then. I'll call again when I get a confirmation number from Western Union."

"'Kay."

"I love you, Sis."

"I love you too."

Revisiting triumph in my role as emotional and financial savior, I strolled to the bank with a pensive gaze fixated no more than ten feet in front of me. With forty minutes to close, I approached the counter and requested to withdraw the necessary amount, leaving my checking account with fifty cents and my saving with exactly one dollar and twenty-*six* cents. As the teller counted, "Two, two-fifty, three, three-fifty," I lost my breath. "Four, four-fifty, five, five-fifty." *If I need* anything *for myself, I'm shit outta luck.* "Six, six-fifty, seven, seven-fifty," my knees became weak. "Eight, eight-fifty, nine. Nine hundred and fifty dollars." *I have nothing.* "Is there anything else I can help you with today?"

Ha...Yeah....

Holding a piece of scratch paper complete with confirmation number, I made my way back to my dorm room, sat and stared at the same obscure gray mark on the wall and turned music on hoping it would quiet the non-stop-talk in my head. I looked at my calendar and counted the number of paychecks I would receive before the semester ended. My eyes focused on the square to the right of today, April 21, imagining the fears, words, and procedures that would occupy that vacant box, wondering what April 22 would come to represent. After fifteen solid minutes of staring at four black lines on a white background, I let *The Warrior Woman* distract my cluttered cognition.

I carried my initial one hundred and one unanswered questions with me to class the next day only, because it was the day *of,* there was actually far more than one hundred and one. For lunch, I decided to avoid the overcrowded food hall on campus. Instead, I walked into town alone to imagine what my sister was enduring without me by her side. Imagining what the space between my sister and mom looked like today. Imagining how far away my dad could set himself emotionally and physically from what was happening.

Along the streets, I could clearly hear the separation of water from tire as cars drove by. The click of fancy shoes on pavement rose and fell as I passed people on the sidewalk. Shallow chitchat hummed about, but my ears were heightened to the sound that youth makes: shrieks, giggles, cries. I walked faster to enter a grown establishment of any kind. I sat myself at the table-for-two by the window in the bookstore to unwind. Staring at the puddle that had accumulated just below the windowsill, I drowned myself in a sea of thoughts and worries.

I closed my eyes and sucked in the longest, slowest breath I ever remember taking, as if the air would enter me and cause all else to exit. I brushed my hands across my face and ran my fingers back through my hair when something small and hard hit my foot. My eyelids popped open and diving under my table chasing a green bouncy ball was a toddler, two, *maybe* three years old. His hair was straight, black, wearing a *Toy Story* t-shirt striped with red, yellow, and white.

"Aiden!" his mom followed behind.

His little eyes lit up as he recovered his prize, "Bowce bah! Bowce bah!" His vibrant smile beamed, revealing two solid dimples embedded in full cheeks.

"Aiden, I told you to put that in your pocket—I'm sorry miss."

"No, you're fine," I assured with a forced smile.

My eyes were locked on his, which sparkled with innocence and life. She took his hand and as soon as they had come, they were gone. *Innocent. Alive. Innocent. Alive.* My thumb anxiously scratched the edge of the cold gray table. Flesh. Metal. Torn. I felt like I had just handed my sister a chance at a bright future with my left hand but ripped a life from her body with my right.

This pain echoed deep within me causing great wars

between goodness and guilt, reason and responsibility, hope and *how could I?* An uncontrollable train of thought roared, but screeched to a loud stop at Shakespeare Station. I instantly hated having read *Macbeth*. Had I not, I'm sure the mental railways would not have configured themselves around the lines, "Will all great Neptune's ocean wash this blood / Clean from my hand?" while I sit and question: *What did I actually pay for?*

The Stereo Typer

By Adrian Jawort

She was the epitome of the starving young artist.

Back in high school, Lydia figured being deemed as a bit odd was a blessing considering the option of being ordinary. Nothing was worse than being ordinary, but now she was less than that because that's all she wanted to be.

She worked at a crappy chain restaurant job, and wasn't even a waitress or hostess. She knew she didn't have the personality to even want to pretend to be annoyingly perky; applied for dishwasher, and would work her way up to cook if she wanted to do better.

But why would she want to do better in that line of work? *This is only temporary,* she continually told herself as she grabbed the stack of hot plates out of the machine. *Before I make it big doing what I love. Fucking A, these are hot!* She forgot she'd taken her gloves off when she went on her brief and interrupted smoke break. But they needed more little plates this time. Little plates they are low on. Always with the plates. Couldn't anyone grab them their damn selves? What about that kid that only stacks the lettuce or whatever the hell he doesn't do? He's worthless and gay in way that didn't make her happy. She personally didn't give two fucks about his sexual orientation, except she knew they wouldn't fire him just because they didn't want to seem discriminatory. The gay kid smiled at her as she walked past him with a stack of plates two feet high. *That kid needs to man up and grab some plates with his limp wrists! That wasn't discriminatory, was it?*

It didn't matter because it was true. She definitely didn't want to make a career out of the restaurant business. She knew she was a writer. Don't let anyone tell you otherwise. Follow your dream. That she would.

Another rejection notice.

She tried to look at the bright side of things: at least they actually replied to her—and quickly. It cut the suspense out. A couple of times they never even replied back, and she hated that worse than a rejection. With rejection at least there was some finality. But she often had the feeling the reader or editor never even bothered to read her short story it came back so fast in the 'form rejection' form. That is, a small printed photocopied piece of paper or copy and paste email saying they "regret having to turn down the submission as it did not fit their current needs"; or having had to open your envelope/email just to send your suck up query extolling the editor and publishers supposed greatness back in your face. It was a waste of time for the postal carriers and email openers, after all. And if she did send it via snail mail, she even had the bargain and privilege of paying for her own self-addressed stamped envelope, or SASE they called it in the writing world. Publishers were shying away from paper, however.

"Stay in school," and "Just Say No" to drugs. Those are the Golden Rules these days for young people to succeed. Lydia went to college, and got busted for having marijuana on her in an essentially illegal search and seizure. But she couldn't fight the charge lest she wanted to sit in jail until the trial date a month later since she wouldn't make bail. She originally plead innocent, but the bitch judge was PMSing and wouldn't let Lydia out on her own recognizance, so she switched her plea to guilty and figured to pay The Man in time payments since she was a working student, but then they wouldn't even let her do that. She'd have to pay the fine in full or sit it out inconveniently right during finals week. Justice is blind to those with possession of a supposedly "dangerous drug."

She got out of jail to a cold reception of nothing. Nothing in her room. It was all in some storage closet by the mail room. No one in the halls. They'd all gone home for the Christmas break. They'd be welcome at home, and be welcomed back the next month, too. Nothing like that for Lydia though. She wouldn't be welcome back, and her parents wanted nothing to do with her. Well, her father hadn't contacted her in three years and he'd left when she was like two. She and her mom hadn't gotten along since she was like...forever. She learned throughout her alcoholic plagued childhood to ignore her mom's discouragement, and even pitied her for her addiction after awhile, but this time she was right: Lydia had amounted to nothing.

"I raised you by myself and you don't appreciate

nothing I ever do for you. Nothing!" That's what her mom said to her the last time they'd spoken. "And now you think you're better than me? Going to some college? You watch now, you won't amount to nothing!"

"I never said I was 'better' than anyone. All I said was don't blame how your life went on me. I'm just sick of it. How you're life is so-o-o fucking bad 'because you had me,'" she mimicked her like the wicked witch she was. "And don't try and hit me, I'm eighteen now."

"Then you can fucking leave the house then if you're 'eighteen,' ungrateful little bitch."

"Fine, I will! And that's what I was doing: packing to get out of this...shithole place." She packed the rest of her belongings and mumbled, "Yeah, I should so-o-o appreciate you bitching to me as usual, just because as usual you got kicked out of the bar for being drunk as—"

"You smart mouth little cunt!" She didn't have time to bring her arms up to defend herself, and was promptly smacked upside the head. It wasn't the first time, but this one was harder than usual and made her see stars. Her mom started raging, punching, and pulling her hair along with a torrent of demonizing words.

No more.

Lydia gave her own mother a hard uppercut to her mouth, and the grip loosened from her hair. After another punch to the her mother's nose, and she grabbed her bags and made way to the door. She never felt so good, so liberated, and so sickened at the same time in her life. She'd defended herself finally, but at what cost? No one should ever hit their own mother like that, no matter what they'd done. Geezus....

She was out the door of her trailer house, and the fresh air awakened her. "And don't you ever come back, ever!" her mom yelled after her, holding her bleeding nose.

"Why would I? I fucking hate you!" she said, instantly regretting it. She wanted to tell her she loved her, just hated her actions. But she didn't need her anymore. Ever. "I don't need anything from you. Anything!" and she meant it. She'd never go back there again.

She went to a park, and cried herself to sleep under a tree that night. It was still okay, she'd be in a dorm room in about a month anyway. She'd have a clean slate, and maybe she'd find a boyfriend with common interests who didn't consider her bizarre and liked her for who she was. She didn't think she looked that bad, really. But that wasn't important, because being a virgin wasn't a social taboo for her regardless of the so-called pressures of modern society to be a dumb whore lest you're presumed some lezbo or Bible freak. What was important was she was on her way to becoming a writer. She was doing something with her life, and her mom was envious and not so subtly made it more or less known in the only way she knew how to do it. Her mom could have been someone as well, but Lydia was born, of course. She wasted her life away raising the ungrateful Lydia.

***

Lydia grabbed her stuff—packed unceremoniously in black garbage bags—off the cold cement floor of the university dorm storage room and walked out into the individualistic snowflakes falling to the ground to conform with the rest of the piles, homeless and more uncertain than ever of where her life would lead her.

Lydia felt as the local bag lady as she trudged with the awkward and embarrassing garbage bags of her belongings, heading towards an apartment complex where she'd sold weed to a chick named Lacey months ago. Selling weed was decent supplemental income for her since high school even when she didn't even smoke it in her frosh and soph years, but now she smoked it at least every few hours if possible. She'd started using it when she was about 16 after someone suggest she finally try it because her weed was 'the bomb' and she could sell it for much more. She ended up smoking entirely too much of it for a beginner that night before she went to bed, and remembered tripping hard and promising to herself she'd never do it again. That promise lasted until the next morning when she woke up still partially buzzed, and liked it as her favorite Nirvana song, "Heart-Shaped Box," melodiously played on her alarm clock. Moderation is good at first, however. Marijuana gave her a reason of sorts to actually want to get up in the morning, like what a coffee drinker must have felt like. She horribly had none on her now.

But she'd stop selling weed when the college semesters started as she didn't want any distractions. She wanted more than anything to succeed in class, and didn't want the inconvenience of stoners continually asking for dime bags messing up her studies. Plus, she was a full-time working student. Was.

She was at the apartment, and had only drifted there because it was fairly close to campus. She'd noticed prior an empty storage closet for the tenants when she nonchalantly checked it the last time she'd been there. She twisted the knob on the closet, and it was still gratefully open and clear aside from some cleaning products. *Thank you, Jesus.*

A middle-aged woman resident was coming out of her apartment, and she knew it would be polite to speak. "Hi! I'm keeping my stuff here for a few days before I leave home. Just got out of college. I know Lacey anyway."

"Oh, no problem," the lady said. "I don't think anyone's ever used that anyway. Does it lock?"

"I don't think so, but there are no valuables. Anyway, can you tell Lacey 'Lydia's stuff is here' whenever you see her, just so she knows? I've got to go somewhere."

She thought Lacey probably was actually home then as it were, so it seemed odd she not tell her herself she was storing her crap there. She wasn't that great of friends with Lacey, but it would have been virtually pointless to tell her about the bags aside from embarrassing herself further by telling her she was now an officially homeless bag lady. Either way, she just wanted to hide from the world and was relieved to retire the bags from her tiring grip.

Of course, Lydia actually didn't have 'to go somewhere' but nowhere as the sun briefly made an appearance from behind the clouds before darting back. The sudden hopelessness of her situation started to well up in her eyes, and make things blurry as she trudged down a slushy alleyway. She was going to cry, but no. She would not be defeated. She could control her feelings. No, she couldn't. Her feelings were as they were, and a tear escaped down her cheek. Lydia wiped it quickly and ashamedly.

Something would make her happy. She had no weed and was supposed to get drug tested anyway, but she did have 15 dollars on her to last until payday in a couple of days. Of course that check would be small too since she never worked all week. She could get drunk. The thought of the daft notion made her smile and giddy, as it was the little things in life that helped you trudge on no matter how bad it got. She felt invigorated.

Lydia did drink a lot for a girl, that she knew. A chip off of the old block like her mother. No, she was nothing like her mother, she always said. Well, at least she thought she handled her alcohol better than her. Calling her own work crossed her mind. She could do that to escape her drudgery and get her mind off the hollowness she was feeling if she wasn't fired, but for some reason the thought of stacking plates just sounded like the worst thing to do. She was half-sure she'd still have her job as they were always desperate for dishwashers, but whatever. They could get along without her for another day. She asked a cell mate of hers that was getting out if she'd call her work and leave a message to tell her boss her whereabouts. It wouldn't have been a first for them considering she noticed a cook or two have the same happen to them.

So her job would theoretically be there for her, much to her slight dismay. She almost wished she'd be fired. Ugh. She ate a microwave burrito from the gas station, bought as much cheap strong beer as she could, and stuffed it into the remaining room of her backpack. Where would she sleep tonight? She could call someone from work and they'd help out—if she went to work. No, keep walking. She'd cross that bridge when she got there, and was incidentally heading towards an actual bridge where she'd figure it out and drink in peace. She cracked a beer, blew the foam off the top of it, and took a mighty slam before sliding the can in her sleeve as to avoid the police's detection of it.

She'd thought about that first cool refreshing drink a few times whilst in jail. Her cellmate had been some methamphetamine addict/tweaker who was oddly entertaining, but she needed to shut up for reals sometimes. She'd been in the hooskal for three months compared to her one week, so whenever she felt like griping she only had to look at the girl yammering across from her to put things in perspective to how bad things could be. Three months in here? Yeesh.

So there was always that to not look forward too, although her one week had pretty much decimated her education prospects for the foreseeable future and that would have consequences lasting longer than three months. She couldn't get out of that hole, hell no. Although she'd gotten nearly perfect marks for almost 3 semesters, she doubted her school would have sympathy to cut her slack for missing finals week on a 'possession of a dangerous drug' charge. Since when was smoking a joint so fucking 'dangerous?'

She thought of her last conversation with her jail cellmate two days ago. "I'm working on my GED at the Adult Ed Center. I think I'll like go to college too after that," Tweaker Girl had said to her. Or, that's what Lydia privately referred to her as. "Maybe I'll like see you there?"

Lydia looked up from the little New Testament she was reading. She got it after going to a Bible study class just to get out of that cell she spent most of the day in where she was alone all day—which suited her fine considering the constant chattering of her cellmate when she was around. They let Tweaker Girl have a job because she had to do real time, and she was always gone somewhere outside picking up trash or whatever. "Uh...yeah. Hopefully. I don't know if they'll let me back in school though."

Not to be negative, but she seriously doubted that Ms. Tweaker would straighten her life out enough to go into college. Oh well. It sounded cool to her, so let her believe it.

"Oh, God, that sucks for you. You're like a poor baby! I'm so sorry, that's gotta blow hard!" Tweaker Girl said.

"Like Hurricane Katrina and a crack whore of the same name, and maybe this dame to blame all the lame same."

"Hah! You thought about that one, huh?"

"Meh...not really. Bizarre filth...just spews forth from thine own tongue, as that its will be done."

Tweaker Girl laughed, let her hair go wild, and started

head banging and singing The Scorpions "Rock me like a Hurricane," song. She said, "You're such a trip! We so need to hang out on the outside! Anyway like that stupid song is like stuck in my head. I heard that on the guard's radio when we went out earlier."

"Is that what it says? That 80's song? 'Rock me,' and not 'raunchy?' It always sounds like they say 'raunchy' to me for some reason. Funny."

"I'm so jazzed. I get out in...uh...six motherfucking hours, bitch! It was nice meeting you, dude, and I'll give you my dinner tonight. I won't need it. I'm going to go and eat a whole pizza or something as soon as I leave. Oh, and I'll call your work to let them know where you are. Thought I'd forget, eh?"

"Not really," she said. "I get out in 2 days. Monday morning sometime. I'm so screwed when I get out. I don't want to think about it."

***

She had gotten out right prior to noon, and didn't get to eat lunch in the jail. Well, at least she could get some real food finally, she'd figured. But a gas station microwave burrito wasn't that much more nourishing.

Now it was about four hours until it got dark out, so that was good because it would not get too freezing until then. It was cloudy, but really not all that cold as the snow came in light flurries every few minutes. So she'd ended up under the bridge of all places, and made a comfortable spot to enjoy her many beverages stuffed in her backpack. Little ice chunks streamed downstream until they thawed and dissipated with the bloodline artery that was the river to replenish the Earth's life. Maybe it even reached the final destination of the mighty ocean she'd never seen, as if that were its light at the end of the tunnel. Or perhaps they got sucked into a pipe that went into the sewer.

Then she saw it: it was a rope dangling from under the bridge that people used to swing and dive into the river with during the warmer months. She was barely feeling the alcohol effects, but the oddest thought crept into her head. She got up, tied the rope into a noose, and swung it toward the river. She almost slipped grabbing it on the swing back.

A passing thought, *I should do it, you know?* She should hang herself. Hell wasn't a deterrent. Life sure as hell certainly wasn't, either. Atheists say there is nothing on the other side which would make life pointless aside from material pleasure and satisfying lusts. There would be no afterlife accountability, just inconvenience for the living to get rid of her soulless body. Hitler never got in trouble after he committed suicide in his bunker. She sat down and pondered this urge.

She wouldn't give up that easily, would she? It was only school she failed out of, and it was only like five stories that had failed to get published. She could re-send them out. She'd been published so far in the school's magazine that they put out yearly at least, but she didn't think that counted for much. Her creative writing professor and English teachers had said she was talented, but almost sort of too disturbing.

Well, for their taste. They even collectively asked her if she needed to see a counselor. But the thing was, she did feel abashed when she handed in her work at times; like she was realizing something about her own soul as she wrote it, and was exposing that to whoever would read it even if the characters did not seem remotely like her.

Lydia felt perturbed, and wanted to be 'normal' for at least one day. She wanted to escape, and was even jealous of those boring, typical preppy girls for the first time. They'd be with their friends driving meticulously clean cars, fresh from lunch from a place of their debated choosing listening to generic top 40 radio pop music while on their way to the mall right now, chatting about trivial inane gossip before going home to a delicious home cooked warm family meal prepared by their loving mothers. Home. Just thinking about the rest of her crappy life was extremely harrowing, because instead of living in a weekly motel room for a month until school started again, she'd be forced to live there for...longer. She'd even be homeless for a few more days before she'd get a new paycheck. She cursed, and even the beer lost it's good taste—not that cheap beer tasted all that great in the first place. Screw it, just do it, you know? Most normal girls attempted suicide as lame cries for help and never succeeded, but she wasn't like them.

Lydia brought out a notebook, and her possessed hand scribbled some words in it. Her notebook and typing on a computer was her only companion, confidante, and counselor. She'd been wanting a boyfriend more and more as the school year went on—not a mere lay. But when she barely had time for herself with her full work and school schedule, it was hard to have an active social life. Plus, it was hard to be social when one was a socially awkward introvert. The minute she tried to be herself, it always weirded people out save for maybe druggies who got a kick out of her eccentricities, so she mostly stayed silent around people.

It would've been worth it to be so lonely if she'd continued getting the good grades she'd been getting. Now it was all worthless. She read her fresh writing out loud as it echoed under the bridge:

"The person was a suicide.... They wanted to take the final ride...see what's on the other side....

"Maybe it's fucked up...maybe it's selfish...but we're not them...hurt again and again.

"The Lotus-Eaters beckon...forever."

She chuckled. What a lovely poem to die to. It sounded almost like a fricken sad alternative rock song more than a poem. She couldn't help that her poems rhymed even on a spur of the moment piece, but wished they didn't so they'd sound more supposedly literary. She'd made up her mind. With a surge of confidence she approached the rope, unceremoniously tightened it around her neck, and stood on a higher rock off to the side. After she swung she'd have nothing to get any footing on, she estimated. Hopefully she'd have a clean neck break if she jumped high enough. Prolonged strangulation wouldn't be fun otherwise.

Lydia closed her eyes and prepared herself. This was it. Don't wuss out and be like those 'other girls.'

Ready...one...two...three...and—wait! She wondered who would find her swinging away or dangling under the bridge. Maybe it would be a kid. It would scare and scar them for life. *Over the river and under the bridge, she'll dangle in the snow!* Oh well, that's life. You die, you know? Hate to break the secret. She bent her knees...deep breath...exhale...ready and—

Wait! You have to at least drink the beer up. It's cold and it'd be a waste. Not to mention it'd look like you were a mere 'failed alki' like your mother in that you couldn't handle your beer just because you got buzzed and turned suicidal.

Life was looking better for the worse. She'd live to die another day and maybe even write about it—just not home to mom.

Off the Path

The Education of Little Man False Star Boy
By Sterling HolyWhiteMountain

That was the summer I got the one and only claim check of my life and spent my own small piece of the Sweetgrass Hills. That was the summer I let June begin to become a memory. That was the summer my uncle told me stories, stone sober and believing wholly in the power of Christ since '72. That was the summer Lorrie Johnson caught June's man Narcisse Bad Strike screwing Alana Morris in his truck well after midnight—in front of June's house—Ho, his truck was just rocking, said Lorrie, when she told the story later to anyone who wanted to listen, although she pretended it was an awful thing to talk about, her best friend's man cheating on her like that with Alana, who everybody knew opened her legs for anyone who came looking. But only a few of us knew Narcisse was chippying off and on with Alana since June had gone home early (too much BV too quick) from Lila Last Dog's New Year's Eve party at Lila's grandpa's house, her grandpa who was closing in on the end of his last term as council chairman after 30 years of thieving with the best of them. We kept the secret of their chippying close to our hearts, each for his and her own reasons, but always because we had some kind of final allegiance to June, or the idea of

June. And all of us benefited from being near her, the way one benefits from having been in the same photograph with a professional athlete, or rising-star politician. We knew June outside the frame of the photo, we had hugged her, laughed with her, I had breathed in her perfume sitting next to her in the bleachers in the morning before classes started and wanted to put my hand between her legs, which I did instead to Kim Big Bear, a small girl with a pretty smile who didn't get the kind of attention she wanted or should have.

What I remember about cashing that check is the teller at the bank. She was a beautiful white girl I wouldn't realize was beautiful until I remembered many years later her icy blue eyes—anything could happen behind those eyes, and in that way she was the perfect accomplice to my crime. I have wondered if she has ever thought about me—had she ever thought of me when she was fucking? Stranger, less beautiful things have happened in the history of the world. My grandpa waited in the truck, the day in Silver Falls was bitter as it should have been, spring was taking its times, with bitter winds blowing down the bitter, emptying streets of old downtown. June sat behind me in a chair in the waiting area, her long legs crossed, her long black hair pushed back behind her ears and splashed over her shoulders—impatient, bored, selfish, indifferent, a younger, less beaten version of the bitch she would be in the coming years, when her beauty fell away in pieces, backhand by backhand, only to be replaced by a meanness wholly commensurate with her once flawless face, her unchipped, unabsent, and perfect white teeth. Fuck, she said, I thought that white girl wasn't gonna give you that money. I thought we was gonna have to beat the piss out of her. She laughed. Her fingers were long and graceful, her nails long and painted purple—but, like most Blackfeet women, that did not mean she did not know how to fight.

On the way to the dealership I held the multiple envelopes within which the rubber-banded hundreds were stacked. Not ever in my life or ever again would I hold 20,000 dollars cash in my hands. There was a black Bronco I'd seen a few weeks earlier, on a similar trip to Silver Falls, when I'd been to the same bank with June, and she had cashed her own check, on her own birthday. We were born only weeks apart, in the spring of 1972, in the old wing of the LaFleur IHS, the wing since converted to the diabetes center where people go when the only thing left them is dialysis, where kind women with gloved hands hook you up to the machine that cleans your blood so you can have a few more conversations with the people you love before you go. June had bought herself an orange Camaro with flames on the driver's side and fat rear tires. The tint on the windows was peeling at the edges, and the black leather gearshift grip was worn smooth and gray and frayed at the edges. She had hung an eagle feather from the mirror—no one did that in those days, people hung furry dice or air fresheners or crucifixes and rosary beads but no one hung feathers from mirrors, it was an anomaly, that large feather, its stalk beaded in LaFleur colors, hung by a leather string, the feather's tip brushing the black vinyl dash when she turned corners cruising around LaFleur. On the way to the dealership, passing fast food restaurants that don't exist anymore, their buildings since reinhabited like snail shells by local insurance companies, by salons with names like Nails & Hair 4 U, by Mexican restaurants run by honest-to-god Mexicans from the real Mexico, people come to Montana to seek their piece of America, auto parts stores that are still auto parts stores, blocks of housing that suggest time passes slower in some pockets of the world—on the way there my grandpa was quiet and June sat between us. I handed over the cash, counting out the hundreds carelessly, like I could count them out forever and there would always be more in that envelope, I don't think the salesman thought I was for real. Until then he had treated the three of us like we had pulled into the lot asking for change to get us home. My grandpa had different kinds of quiet—sometimes because he didn't want to talk, sometimes because he was waiting for the right time to speak, and sometimes because if he spoke he might start a fistfight. He was not afraid of anyone, so far as I knew, and though he was at least 20 years older than the salesman he would have had no trouble with him—you can tell a man who is a fighter from one who is not from one look in his eyes. The salesman with his curly brown hair and brown mustache and round face talked tough but only his words seemed strong, he was not rez tough, if you looked past the curtain of what he said there was no wizard pulling the levers, there was only an absence of presence, a pale mockery of being. When he handed me the keys he was already looking away, he didn't shake my hand, he was watching June and her stonewashed jeans as we walked out of the dealership. You're a rich man, my grandpa said, looking at me as though I were the only other person in the Silver Falls, as though Silver Falls did not exist at all, in fact, and we were standing on an ancient plain with only the wind as our companion. I bet you feel like you could do anything, enit. He set his hand on my shoulder. He was right. I felt invincible.

So we drank. We drank like there was no today. We drank whatever we wanted. We drank in the morning, we drank in the late morning, we drank in the early afternoon, we drank in the afternoon, we drank in the late afternoon, we drank in the early evening, we drank in the evening, we drank when the sun went down behind the mountains, we drank in the dark under myriad stars our great-great-great grandparents had called our relatives. June got back with Narcisse for one night at a party and the two days following and then he was back with Alana going to rodeos with her and living off her winnings. Narcisse, who weaved in and out of our summer like a bird flying through an aspen grove. Narcisse, who was long and lean and pale ochre and had those blue-green Cree eyes that looked beyond everything to what he wanted. I was a little shorter, thinner (in those days), darker, was not a ball player, was not the one whose photo was in the paper for four years of varsity basketball, football, track, was not the one who had captured June the summer before she started high school. I had decent grades. I was funny. I was an alternate on the cross-country team that won the state championship three years consecutive. My teachers liked me. None of these things were enough. Over the coming three months I broke hundreds as often as the federal government broke promises. On the way home from Silver Falls in my Bronco me and June had made an agreement—we would take turns buying. We made this deal knowing in reality I would buy three times for her every one. We made this deal knowing we were not old enough to buy but knowing if LaFleur is anything it is an easy place to find a runner. We made this deal knowing it was impossible we wouldn't live forever.

Here is what we drank: Boone's (peach for me, strawberry for June, strawberry-banana on Tuesdays and full moons); Miller Light, 12 pack; Bud Light, 12 pack; Budweiser, 12 pack; Mickeys but only in bottles because they were not sold in cans then; MD 20/20 in any flavor they had in stock, although my preference was for grape, the poisonous aftertaste of the cheap liquor was best masked by the artificial grape flavoring. The first time we drank Mad Dog we had bought three bottles, grape, strawberry, and banana—the first two our respective choices, the last because, as June said, Better get another just in case, you know? We drove up to Midvale where all the white people on the rez lived and we sat in front of the laundromat just beyond the circle of light projected by the street light and drank. The stars blazed. Fuck this is a weird town, she said, nothing but white people here. I nodded and drank. You ever wonder what it's like to be white? she said. I nodded and drank. Tommy Davis, a white friend of ours who was cruising around with us that night, who had been in school with us since kindergarten, who had spent almost every day of his life in La Fleur, said, It ain't that great being white. He grabbed the bottle of grape from me and drank. In the half-light you could see the scar that ran from the right edge of his mouth almost back to his ear. He had a black eye from his latest fight with his older brother. June peered at him through the dark and her drunkenness. Ho, she said, I plum forgot you were white. We laughed and passed what was left of the grape around. The next morning June called me to ask what had happened to the driver's side door of her Camaro—there was a scrape all the way down the side, exposed metallic streaks showed through the flames on the door. No idea, I said. Weren't you the one driving? she said. I guess, I said. We laughed.

We drank whatever was around wherever we were. That first month of summer there were keggers every weekend, sometimes during the week, tire fires lit in the countryside, the cheapest, piss-tasting beer you can imagine passed out in red or blue plastic cups, emptied and tossed into the dark plains night or into the fire, its forked flames licking the darkness above—the tribal police flashing their lights as they pulled up to the party, kids scattering into the dark and the hills and the trees like spirits disturbed from their revelry; trailer parties full of kids we'd gone to school with and people we didn't know: slick, city cousins visiting from Seattle, Oakland, Portland—for example, Misty La Croix's new boyfriend from Tahlequah, one of those pretty Indian men looking like he just stepped out of an ad in a magazine, a drawling Indian with braids and an aura of beautiful invincibility who left Misty and one of her cousins pregnant after only two weeks in LaFleur; for example, Londa Williams, Ron Fitz's cousin from Calgary, who for all of three seconds sat alone and beautiful as a dark star on a couch at Tiny Cardinal's house party before three guys were around her like bees around a flower and my chance to speak to her was gone; for example my cousin Calvin Kills Last who had lived most of his life in the Berkeley area and brought with him all the city cool that drove more than a few (including me) to accuse him of acting too good—an accusation that was ended following his smoking a bunch of us out til people were teasing each other about being more Asian than Indian, and also when a few nights later he'd gotten into a fight with Roland Schultz and managed to take him to a draw. I drove them both to the ER, Calvin's broken nose, and Roland's broken and cut-up hand bleeding all over my seats even though both of them had taken their shirts off in an attempt to stop just that from happening—Calvin holding his bunched-up shirt to his nose, Roland wrapping his around his hand. Calvin's last words to me, before he went back to California never to return? Calvin who looked so much like our great-grandpa Yellow Strong Bull Ribs you felt, sometimes, at moments, you were talking to a ghost? Calvin, who would make something of a career for himself as a bit actor in films needing *Native-American-looking actors*? Fuck all you rezzers, he said, when me and our cousin Vance Lost His Gun dropped him off at the Silver Falls airport—you're a bunch of ignorant pricks.

Off the Path

The first person from our class to die was Arnell Reeves. He passed out at the wheel one night on the way back from a bar just off the reservation in Blood Creek and rolled his uncle's truck 8 times before being thrown through the windshield. He died en route to IHS. He was sober. The next person to die was Shirley Red—I can't remember her last name, everyone had always called her Shirley Red or Shirl Red or Red (her hair was black)—when she and her friends rolled her truck outside of LaFleur going west on their way to Starr School. The other two girls riding with her broke ribs and forearms and whatnot, one was severely concussed and the other was briefly in a coma, her relatives sitting by her in the hospital room that whole week, the room smelling of that odd combination you will sometimes run into at IHS: sage, sweetgrass, sweet pine, leather, cigarettes, antiseptic, bodies. Red's funeral was closed casket because of the damage done to her face when she was thrown from the truck. The next to die was Harlan Grass. He was walking along side the road when someone driving around 50 mph swiped him with their door and knocked him into the ditch where he lay for at least 12 hours in what was probably excruciating pain, his spine snapped and his left ribs, arm, shoulder, shoulder blade, clavicle, and hip broken, any number of people passing him without stopping because, as the woman said who finally stopped, He just looked like some old clothes and some trash way down there in the ditch by the trees. The old men who sat together and drank coffee at the Red Bird (before it closed in the late 90s) in the mornings talked about how awful it must have been for that boy to lay there like that. They discussed the fact that Harlan had been drunk himself (.012 BAC), so maybe he had been staggering in to the middle of the road himself. Maybe he had not been doored at all. They discussed the similarly tragic deaths of friends and family they still missed and more than one of them wondered to himself if he would see these same relations and friends in his dreams, as the old people had used to say would happen when your time was drawing close. It was also rumored that the woman who found Harlan must have either been in the vehicle that hit him or knew the people who did it because how else would she have found him, way down there in the ditch by the trees? Nothing came of these rumors. Harlan's family denounced the tribal police for being utterly inept, an altogether un-new accusation. After that third funeral in less then a month I determined in some deep and unassailable part of myself that if I had to die—a fact I was not convinced of just yet—I was not going to die because I was drinking. That night as a way of saying goodbye to Harlan me and June and a few others grabbed some sixers and a few bottles of Boones and partied in an abandoned trailer way out north of LaFleur. Around three in the morning when the air had become cool from air drafting off of the creek nearby, someone lit the trailer on fire and though it was not my trailer and belonged to no member of my family I felt like I had lost a rib. We laughed nervously for a while and when our worry that the cops would catch us there became too great we piled into June's Camaro and headed for town. After we had dropped the others off and we were parked in front of my house June told me Narcisse wanted to get back with her because he realized he had made a mistake and he missed her—also it turned out Alana had been with another guy the whole time, a white guy from Chariton who was a champion bronc rider and was 30 years old and had his own ranch and everything. I told June she would be stupid to take him back, he was just going to do the same thing to her again. I told her she should get with me, I would treat her right and we would be happy together. She laughed at me and told me she didn't think of me that way at all. You're my best friend, she said. I can't even imagine kissing you. I leaned over and kissed her. She pushed my face away and told me to get out. I told her I wasn't getting out until she promised me she wasn't getting back with Narcisse. Don't tell me what to do, she said. I'll tell you whatever I want, I said. Who are you right now? she said. The new me, I said. When I got to my room I lay in bed and counted my money. I put the envelopes with the hundreds I had not spent back under my boxspring and until I fell asleep I thought about things that had nothing to do with loss or time or misfortune because in truth they were as unfamiliar to me as my own face would be decades down the road.

In July the rain clouds fell away and the sun blazed and the plains became a pale brown in the heat and the hot breeze. On the 4th we attended Jackson Hunter's funeral—he had rolled his red Blazer five times on the way out of LaFleur running from the tribal cops. It wasn't uncommon to see two or three or four tribal law enforcement vehicles chasing someone through town at high speed, their spinning red lights cutting the reservation dark in succession like arcing spirits momentarily illuminating the dark chambers of hell. That night while we sat around a fire and people told stories about Jackson if they felt like it and stayed silent if they felt like it and laughed if they felt like it. Ginger Hunter, Jackson's cousin through both his dad and his mom, cried uncontrollably. She had started by telling us she couldn't believe it she couldn't believe it she couldn't believe he was gone and fell apart from there. I sat by her and put my arm around her and she leaned into me hard, pushing the side of her face into my armpit. The wetness of her tears and snot and saliva soaked through my shirt. We had been in school together since kindergarten. When we were kids, before her dad was elected to council and secured a house for his family in one of the newer housing projects on the north end of LaFleur, we had been neighbors, and me and her had played in the mud between our houses any number of afternoons in the spring and in the fall, and though my memory is imperfect I'm sure she was the first girl I held hands with. On the way home I blacked out and drove into the ditch and back out and across the highway and swervingly returned to our lane although I have no memory of it. What I remember are screams coming to me as if from a great distance, like screams crossing a black river. The next afternoon me and June met up and we drove to Blood Creek and ate lunch at Taco Juan's. We sat in the back in the hard, orange booths and vacillated between saying we couldn't believe how many friends we had lost since graduation, and telling rugged jokes about how we wouldn't be getting any of the money back they owed us.

Then it was powwow time—that time of year when so many of our dislocated relatives came back to the reservation to visit along with thousands of non-Indians from all four directions come to see the Indians do what they do best—put on a show for the tourists. For a week the reservation air crackled with the electricity of excitement, the secret cousin of hope. I helped my uncle Khan put up our family's lodge near the north entrance of the dance arbor, where we had been setting up our lodge since before powwow time, since before the coming of the naapikoan, when instead of a dance arbor there had been a massive summer camp on those very grounds, with Nitsitapi coming from hundreds of miles north to participate in the O'kan, to tell stories, to find a man or a woman to be with. Khan always had kids with him, he would teach anyone who wanted to know how to set up a lodge. He would tell the kids why Pikuni started with four poles instead of three. He would say, Don't call it a tipi, that word belongs to those Sioux, call it a *moyis*, it's like saying, 'the circle where we live,'—and the kids would parrot what he said, knowing nothing about how much knowing a single word of the mother tongue would mean to them someday, or that even a single such word in the right mouth at the right moment was enough to expose the shadow of this grand American project.

The last afternoon of the powwow, when we were sitting in the arbor, in the shade of the highest bleacher, Khan said he'd heard from my grandpa (his dad) I'd been drinking a lot.

I drink some, I said. That's not what I heard, he said. I heard you're out every other night with that one. Which one, I said. You know, he said, that one.

We watched the women's fancy competition for a minute, the singers' voices blaring over the PA system—they were down to the last four, the judges standing at the periphery, scrutinizing the women. One of the dancers, she was a Siksika from up by Calgary, I had seen her summers before, her moccasins did not seem to touch the ground, she obeyed the physical laws of another world. The women danced, and my heart ached for reasons that had nothing to do with attraction —I didn't want any of them, I had no interest in speaking to them, I wanted to watch.

While they were announcing the winners Khan looked at me and said, Well, are you getting some or what? I shook my head. I knew better than to show any vulnerability around him—if I did he would come after me like a starving dog after a bone and never stop teasing. Fuck, better find one who'll give it up, he said. Pretty soon you're gonna be too old to use that tiny thing between your legs. We laughed. The afternoon sun looked down with an uninhibited glare. I noticed again, the way you will suddenly notice someone again for the first time, for no particular reason at all, his somewhat Asiatic features, his wispy fu manchu, the smudged lenses of his glasses. That night I lay in our lodge and listened to the sound of kids running between camps, voices drifting through the lazy dark, the rustle of Khan turning over in his sleeping bag. Earlier I had seen June standing in line with Narcisse, waiting to get a brick of fries, leaning on his arm. There had been something beautiful about them, their bodies seemed to belong together in the half-shadows. I had gone up to them and stood next to Narcisse, saying hi to June but not using her name. I asked Narcisse how he was, it had been a while, did he know where the 49 was because I hadn't heard. He didn't say much, he was one of those guys who didn't talk a lot. He half-smiled and gave me that dull look that made you think it was you that was stupid. 49 is out to 7 Mile is what I heard, he said. You going out? I said. Naw, fuck that noise, he said. I asked him what he would do. He shrugged. I'll figure it out later. Bye Little Man, June said, in an overloud voice. Almost angry. I waved my hand without looking back.

A few weeks after the powwow we had attended two more funerals, although this time they had died in the same wreck, way north of LaFleur, on their way into town from a bonfire party up by the Canadian border. One day Greg Young Bear came back from Silver Falls with the names of our dead classmates tattooed to the inside of his left forearm. I laughed at him. Holy fuck that's stupid, I said. I saw that something inside me had begun to go cold. Ho, what the hell did you do that for?June said. He shrugged. He said, Somebody's gotta keep track. Fuck that's fucking fucked up, Kaila Reeves said. Jokes, Greg said. I just woke up yesterday morning in my motel room and had a new tattoo. No refunds on that ish, Kaila said. I leaned in to look at his arm. Two of the names were spelled wrong. Okss, June said. We all laughed. Back in my room I wrote out the names of the dead on a piece of paper. I counted them up and tried to picture each of their faces. I put checks next to the ones who were related to me. I put an x next to the ones who had died in a claim check car.

On the 23rd of July, 1990, I found my grandpa sitting in his truck not seeming to know where he was. The doc at IHS told us he'd had a minor stroke and said, because my grandpa was a *remarkably healthy for a man his age*, that he *would probably recover as much as one can from such a thing*. The doc was large, both tall and wide, and his belly hung over his belt and pushed out his white coat like two white doors forced opened by plaid dough. *Of course, you will have to keep him from smoking*. Like he was talking about a child. I stopped drinking and spent most of my time at home with my grandpa. Daily we would go up to IHS for his physical therapy. At first I would lean against one of the counters in the PT room, watching the therapist (she was a woman from Dine' country, as I remember) talk to my grandpa in a smooth, soothing voice while she helped him struggle through his exercises. Though the struggle to step into the shadow of who he'd been barely registered on his face, because he so rarely showed any sign of suffering or difficulty those small indicators cut through me like the finest of blades. After those first few days I would wait in the lobby and read old copies of Sport Illustrated, poring over them as though some secret between the well-handled covers would release me from whatever my life had become. I thought about how many classmates we had lost already—there was no feeling, just an open space in my head like a question mark. At night after helping him to bed and making sure he had a cup of water next to his bed in case he woke and was thirsty I would go out to the living room and watch TV without watching it and after he had fallen asleep I would bring a folding chair into his bedroom and sit there watching him breathe until I fell asleep sitting up or lay on the floor and fell asleep using a couch cushion as a pillow. I did not fall asleep or wake up thinking about June.

The first time my grandpa woke up and found me on his bedroom floor he told me to go to my room. I did. The next time he woke and found me sitting in the folding chair in the dark he told me to go to my room. I did. The next time he told me to go to my room I said I wouldn't. My boy, he said, you got to rest. I said I didn't. He looked old and weak, lying on his back with the covers up to his chest. The next afternoon we were sitting in the kitchen at the table. He had just told me it would be a good thing if I got him some cigarettes. No, I said. He looked more disappointed than angry, like a boy who had been refused a ball. He said to tell him about what was going on with the new council members. Elections were last summer, I said. He looked off, toward the kitchen window that looked west onto the unfurling plains—out there was the answer to his problem. How about this, he said, tell me that *Katoyisiks* one. I started and stopped and started again. I rubbed my palms against my eyelids. I can't remember those old stories, I said. Lawrence, he said, you need to get some beauty rest pretty bad. If you don't none of those women are gonna love you. I laughed. He had not told a joke that I could remember since I'd found him in his truck. A few tears I didn't expect ran down my face. I wiped them away. I think I'll be around for a while yet, he said. I've been known to be one tough injun. I laughed again. I wiped more tears from my face.

It was true that he did recover. It was also true that he did not recover. He was not who he was before (but when are we?)—there were no obvious, external indicators, it was not one of those strokes that paralyzed one side of his face or body, he had all his former speech capabilities, as far as his movement went there was the slightest shuffle to his gait that, if you were not paying close attention or did not know him before, you might have confused for a limp, maybe an old rodeo injury, or an injury from his time in the service, or even an injury from when he played basketball for the old catholic school that burned down before I was born. Even those who knew him relatively well but did not see him very often might not notice—I was not one of those people. The ever-so-slight fuzziness, that almost imperceptible hesitation that surrounded him like a golden haze—it cut me again and again, as if I had never been cut that way before, as if I were losing the love of my life each time.

I wasn't tired only because of my bedside vigils—not long after the powwow I had run into Amber Spotted Horse while in the IHS lobby. The first time I saw her she flashed a smile at me and waved, and gave me this look like she was looking at something she had never seen before, or was seeing something familiar in a new way, the way you will sometimes look at yourself in the mirror when you are drunk or high and see your face as others might see it, like it finally belongs to someone else. I didn't know what the look was but I felt it in my chest. A woman can give you a look like that and for a few minutes all the power in the universe belongs to you. She must have been around 27. She had a kid with my cousin James False Star, who was between me and Amber in age. He was one of those stunningly good looking men who looked the way both white people and Indians wanted Indians to look. When I was a freshman in high school and James was a senior Amber had come after him pretty hard one Christmas break when she was home from college and at the end of the next summer she had their son. The jokes in the locker room earlier that spring were James had really broke that horse, enit, or how long would it be before Amber foaled out, etc. Amber was recently single during that time when I was taking my grandpa to PT.

Amber showed me any number of things I had never thought or dreamed about knowing. My back was strong and straight with her at my side. We were rarely together in public. She did not want it. Though James and I were cousins he was not so much my cousin that he wouldn't fight me over Amber. Not because he still had feelings for Amber—he had never had any real feelings for her, other than the feeling he got in his dick when they were together, and the excitement and pride he felt knowing a woman who was the subject of more than a few locker room and cruising-main conversations was the one underneath him and on top of him and in front of him and lying by his side later when it was done. But also because James was one of those pricks who would fight sometimes just to fight. Being around him was like being around a wild horse—you had no idea if he was going to eat out of your hand or kick you in the chest. If he was drinking it was most likely the latter. That was what Amber told me, anyway, at the time—she didn't want any drama with James, who had already fought a few other guys she had dated since he left her for Georgia Brings Night (and this only a few weeks after he got Amber pregnant). He's such a fucking little boy, she would say, sometimes, when we'd just finished and I could still feel my heart beating. What about me? I once said. I tried to sound like I was joking, but it was an honest question I didn't expect to ask—being with a woman that much older than you will make you doubt yourself in ways you never would otherwise. This isn't that serious, she said. She got out of bed and went into the bathroom. She sat on the toilet and looked at me while she peed. You really have no idea about anything, do you, she said, and laughed.

When we did go out I paid. I insisted. Something about being with Amber made me feel a need to be responsible. I felt myself reaching not to be an older Little Man but an older Lawrence False Star Boy, the full name, not the abbreviated name, lacking Boy or even Star (some of my friends had nicknamed me False when we were freshman). Amber had even said once, early on, You're stupid for wanting to pay for me, you should be saving that money. Do you even have a bank account? But she did let me, because the truth is very few people will refuse such generosity, even if they know you are making a mistake in being generous. Mostly in the evenings we would go out to St. Mary, where there were restaurants only open in the summer, and because of the prices it was a mostly tourist crowd. I wasn't bothered that she didn't want to be seen with me around other Blackfeet—it was enough to walk into a place and have people look at the two of us, to see men staring at her and then looking at me with contempt. In some vaguely acknowledged chamber of my heart I knew she was using me in some way I didn't understand, and that was fine. We used each other.

One time we went to the Fire Station, a restaurant 40 miles east of LaFleur. June and one of her friends were there. She couldn't stop looking at us. We were both dressed well, I was wearing slacks and a button down shirt, dress shoes that shone in the dim restaurant light. Amber wore a black skirt and a blue top and black high heels, her black hair straight and pushed back behind one ear. We had bought the clothes together, and Amber had picked out mine. Amber ordered the highest priced bottle of wine. She ordered some kind of seafood dish I had never heard of, the most expensive item on the menu other than the wine. I wasn't particularly interested in being there that night, the summer Olympics were on, and my grandpa was watching the sprint semi-finals. I had wanted to watch it with him, but when Amber had called that afternoon she had spoken to me in a that particular voice she used when she wanted something, and who was I to say no? Let's get dressed up and go eat, she said. Then later you can screw me however you want. So I went, and felt an echoing guilt behind my ribs that colored the whole night like a sunset that stretched across the sky, because I could tell my grandpa had wanted me to stay. I also went knowing full well what she said was a lie—she would tell me how she wanted it done, and I would do it. To get my thoughts away from my grandpa, I leaned in toward Amber, I laughed, I smiled, I didn't look once in June's direction. When we left I spit on June's orange Camaro. Why did you do that? Amber said. Because I felt like it, I said.

Another time I drove us to Silver Falls. The right side of my Bronco's back bumper was smashed in by then a result of a quick departure from a party a few weeks earlier. Amber talked about it incessantly, she couldn't get it out of her head. The whole night she talked about how shamed she was to be driving around in a car as beat up as mine. She had been on my ass of late, for no particular reason as far as I could tell. There was also the fact of the passenger side door, dented pretty good from a party a few nights before. My cousin Rico had borrowed it; he couldn't remember what happened, maybe it was Greg LaCroix that had backed into it, maybe it was Shelley Reeves had done it, maybe he had hit a horse on his way back to the highway. Either way Rico felt so bad about it he avoided me for the next year, turning the other way if we were walking toward each other in a public place, acting like he didn't see me if we drove past each other on Iniiwa. She kept at it the whole night, what was she doing with a kid who drove a beat up Bronco, what did people think about her walking around with a kid, Sometimes I just feel stupid in public with you. When I was on top her that night, in the cheap hotel room on east edge of Silver Falls, the one with only fifteen units and a partially burned out neon that sign that said, simply, Motel, she started talking—she told me it would be better if I had a bigger dick. She told it would better if I were older. She told me it would better if I weren't such a pussy. She told it would be better if I was James. Most of it didn't make any sense. I told her not to talk to me that way but she kept going. She started pushing me off of her. I said what the fuck was she doing? We're gonna play a game, she said. I'll push you away and you're not gonna let me do it. Before I could say anything she pushed hard against my chest. She tried to pull her hips away from me. She slammed her palm into my jaw. Rage washed over me like a beautiful aura. The next morning she waited in the car, her sunglasses covering the light bruise under one eye, while I paid for the room. My jaw was still sore. On the way home we hardly talked; we had crossed some kind of threshold and I didn't know what there was to say about it, except that I had liked it.

That night after I'd helped my grandpa to bed I watched TV and got bored and went over to Theo Galvin's. June was there. I didn't try to talk to her; I acted as if she didn't exist; a week earlier she had gotten engaged to Narcisse and hadn't even told me about. When she finally sat by me on the couch, a bottle of Beam in her hand, she told me I looked different. You look engaged, I said. Yeah, I guess so, she said. Well, are you happy or what? I said. She was drunk enough to be honest. She looked confused, wide-eyed, like a child exposed to a new environment. Fuck, I don't know, she said. Why you being so mean to me lately? she said. We haven't even talked in forever. I ain't being mean, I said, I'm just being honest. Ho, she said. You're my best friend. I didn't say anything. I looked around the room, at the people, the military photos of multiple generations of Galvin men and women. Those girls over there aren't even in high school yet, I said. We used to go to parties when were that age, June said. I guess, I said. I went home and looked at myself in the mirror —I had grown two inches in the past two months, I was lean, dark from the sun. Summer was closing down. I wondered what it would be like to die.

The last weekend of August I was hanging out with Khan at his place on the edge of old low rent. His house was spare: a photo of him a few years earlier at a barbecue with some of our relative tacked to the kitchen wall, a single dial radio sitting on a wood box in the living room next to a ragged easy chair that had used to belong to my grandpa when I was a kid, blankets hung from the upper corners of the windows, blankets he would pin up at night to keep anyone from looking in. We sat at the kitchen table and drank coffee. After we'd talked for a while, and he had teased me about Amber—I bet she's just training you good, enit—I made a comment about how all anyone wanted me to do was give them money. Our cousins have bummed me, June had me paying for everything, and now Amber's got me paying for everything, I said. These guys are using me like a ATM. I smiled. I felt stupid and sorry for myself. Khan was serious. Your grandpa ever tell you what that check you got was for? I shook my head. He looked directly at me, something he never did. He started talking, and even though I didn't want to hear anything he said, I knew I had to listen. Well you know our first reservation was a lot bigger than this one, he said. Almost all the way out to the edge of the state in the northern part. All those towns along Highway 2? Those are all on our land. Those other three reservations, they're on our land too. If you go into North Dakota, just on the other side of the border, there's a museum built where the first traders that came to meet with us went, that was as far west as they could come. Think about that! he said. All the way over there! And now here we are, on this little bit here. I took a long breath. I had heard this land bullshit before. I was thinking how Amber looked like the night before when I had put my hands around her neck...—and so our land was took in that 1886 agreement and we never got paid for it. See, thing about these agreements is they're only as good as both sides making the agreement. So you know the Sweetgrass Hills, right? Of course, I said. I was irritated. They were hills to east of our reservation, and the older people talked about them with great reverence. I had only been out there two times in my life —once with my grandparents, when gram was still alive, and I was a little boy, and once earlier in the summer, with some friends. We had taken some tires out there and lit them on fire and drank cheap whiskey. I had told June I loved her, and she had laughed. A week later you could still see smoke rising from that spot a mile off the highway. Well those hills, he said, calling them sweetgrass is a mistake. They're actually Sweet Pine Hills. Cause those ceremonial people use sweet pine, and that's were you could go to get it. *Katoyisiks*—that's how you say it in the language. I repeated the name to myself, silently. So here's the thing—that money you got is for those hills. He pointed east, with his hand on the back of which was a crudely tattooed crucifix he had done himself, past the fridge and the house walls and the high school and the edge of LaFleur, across the plains to those hills. Claim checks are settlement money, he said. Money to us from the government, to make up for not paying for all that land the first time. So think of it like this—every cent you spend is you spending your piece of those hills. That's what that money is. Pretty weird, enit. I don't need to hear this, I said. Don't matter if you want to hear it, he said. It's what's true. All you kids getting those claim checks when you turned 18, you're spending those hills. He laughed. There was meanness in his laughter. I went home and, despite myself, counted out what money I had left. There was less than I expected. That night I cruised around with my cousin Ron Big Bull—he had come down from Canada. He wanted to party, so we did. I didn't drink, and when he asked if he could bum some money I said no. Come on, he said, you're the one with the big check. He laughed. I didn't.

The next time I ran into June I was on my way out of the grocery store. I had a bag in each arm. She stopped me in the middle of the parking lot. I miss you, she said. I been pretty busy, I said. The night before Amber had tied my wrists with a cheap, silk scarf covered in flaming skulls. The skin on my wrists still burned. Let's hang out tonight, she said. Tonight I'm taking the old guy for a drive, I said. Afterwards, then, she said. Fuck, go sober up, I said. You smell rank. Ho, ok then, she said. On the drive back to the house my grandpa said, I haven't seen you with that one for a while. Yeah, I said. You two used to be pretty close, he said. Yeah, I said. You should buy her dinner sometime, he said. I don't like being around her anymore, I said. Well how about that Goes Last girl, he said. She would be a good one to be with. Nah, I said. She was soft-spoken, a shawl dancer, her hair was always in a long braid, a straight-A student, and whenever she laughed she covered her mouth. I thought she was boring. That weekend I saw June again, standing with Narcisse across from me, at Loren Fairchild's funeral. She looked at me and I gave her nothing. The dry wind blew between all of us. I looked at the sky and the high, rising clouds that moved slowly through the blue and the light of the late afternoon told me summer was gone. Though it would be two months yet before we saw snow already our hearts were turning toward the long winter. I saw the openness I had felt only a few months before was the openness of a newborn pup. I had believed the only thing in store for myself was freedom, sunlight, the warm wind.

Not long after the funeral Amber found out she was pregnant. Like most Indians we had no idea what birth control was or why you would use it. Jokes. Amber had told me from the very start to pull out whenever I was close. Don't get me pregnant, Little Man, she would say. I'll fucking kill you if you do. The night she called to tell me I was standing at the window, watching the nuclear sun set. I didn't feel panic—not yet. I felt resentment. I knew exactly when it had happened. A few weeks earlier when I was about to pull out she had told me to stay in her. She had put her hands on my waist, not with her usual harshness but gently, so gently I could not pull away. I want you to come in me, she said. No, I said, but already I was a liar. The first thing she said when my grandpa handed me the phone was, You dumbass, I told you never to come in me. She screamed at me loud enough that I had to go into my bedroom so my grandpa didn't start asking questions. When I asked her what we were going to do she said *we* weren't going to do anything. She said she would make up her mind for herself and she would let me know when she had. You fucking asshole, she said. You fucking fucked up my life. All you fucking False Stars have done is fuck me over. A few days later the old guy asked me what was wrong. I told him. Well, I guess she really likes False Star men, don't she, he said. He laughed. It's not funny! I said. Not much is funny, he said, but you got to laugh anyway. We were quiet. The kitchen clock ticked. You'll be ok, he said.

On one of those sunny, warm, early fall days, those days that are warm enough to remind you of summer, but short enough to tell you summer is as gone for good, I found myself driving by June's. I hadn't seen her for a while. While waiting for Amber to tell me what she was going to do I had hardly left the house. June had called once but I didn't call her back. I let myself in without knocking, the way I always had, expecting to see her mom in the kitchen where she usually was on summer days, but she was not there. I went from room to room to see if anyone was around. When I got to June's I sat on her room bed. I ran my hands over the covers. A journal rested on the floor next to the side of the bed where she usually slept. I flipped open to the last entry.

I don't even know what to do. Narcisse is so handsome but does he really love me?? Now that he's been with those other ones I don't know what to do I feel like a whore when I'm around him like I am just one of his women. And he asked me out of the blue???? And then I heard he was with that one from Blood Creek again at the rodeo in Ft. Hall last weekend. I feel pretty alone right now and mom & dad won't hardly talk to me since I said yes. I can't stay away though.

Welcome to the club, I said, and put the journal down. I lay facedown on her bed and breathed in her smell from her pillow. I unzipped and grabbed the bottle of lotion sitting on her nightstand. I picked up the journal again and opened it to the entry I had just read. I held it in front of me until I came on the pages. Fuck you, I said. My voice was swallowed up by the stuffed animals, the heavy comforter, the old boy band posters on her wall that seemed like they could not possibly have belonged to her. I shut the journal and left the house. I would not talk to June for years many years after that.

With what I had left I bought turkeys for some of the older people around our part of town, the ones I knew didn't have money for something like that. And rolls, and cheese, and potatoes, and bacon, and milk, and eggs. On the day of the first snowfall I tried to give my last hundred to my grandpa. He held his hand out, palm toward me. I don't want nothing to do with that money, he said. Let me pay the phone bill, then, I said. Nope, he said. Go pay somebody else's bills. So I did—I paid my auntie's phone bill, which left me with seventy dollars. I decided to keep the last fifty for myself, and spent the other twenty on a steak dinner at the Red Bird. I had it rare, because there was something sophisticated seeming about a rare steak. I put butter and then more butter on the mashed potatoes, and I put butter on the green beans too. I salted everything. I drank three cokes. I felt like a king eating his last meal. Amber told me that night she was keeping the baby. But I'm not staying with you, she said. I asked why. You're a child, she said. Maybe, I said. Least I got a high school diploma, that's more than you can say for James. I laughed. She didn't laugh. So when are you getting a job? she said. Pretty soon, I guess. That night I went for a walk. A long black cloudbank hung over the mountains—otherwise the sky was clear. A cold, luminescent blue. When I had made it to Government Square my cousin Gerald pulled up next to me in his red Ford, the result of his own claim check spendings. He wanted to party. Nah, I said. Come on, he said, just get in. I shook my head. Just get in, he said, we're going out to Jim's at Bear Head. That was a place on the southeast side of our rez, where people had settled in the 1800s when they didn't want anything to do with the BIA agents.

Once I was got in we did not go straight out—first we stopped at Corey Fish's and then we stopped at Jerry

Houseman's and then we stopped at Wynona Day Bull's place. I got to check on something, Gerald would say, when I asked him what we were doing. And each time Gerald wouldn't let me come in, and each time he came out shaking his head. While we drove we talked about Narcisse and June—the wedding date had been set for next summer. Did you ever get a piece of that? he said. Nope, I said. Then we talked about Rhonda Green and Glen Hawk breaking up. Then Amber. You've been with that one for a while, Gerald said. I bet that's been fun. Yeah, I said, it's been fun. It's over now. Nah, man, you gotta ride that horse til it drops. He laughed. I looked out the window. Then we talked about some of the parties we'd been to earlier in the summer, Gerald doing most of the talking. By now we were cruising up and down Iniiwa, not even trying to go toward Bear Head. When we got set for our fourth trip down the strip I held up my hand. Just go to my place, I said. He feigned surprised and nodded his head. On the way there I said, You're such fucking asshole. What? he said. When we got to my house I went in and checked to see was my grandpa sleeping ok. He was, lying in bed with pillows propping up his chest and shoulders and head. He took long, slow breaths. In my room I grabbed the fifty from under the mattress. When I got back in the truck I crumpled up the bill and threw it in Gerald's face. Here you go, you prick, I said. That's all I got left. He frowned for a second, still acting like he didn't know what was going on. Bro, I'll get you back for it, he said. He picked up the bill, and smoothed it against the steering wheel. Don't worry about it, I said. I don't want it anymore. He smiled his huge smile. Now that's a good Indin, he said.

The End

ABOUT THE AUTHORS

Cinnamon Spear is a Northern Cheyenne woman, writer, and documentary filmmaker. She was raised in a large family on the reservation in Lame Deer, Montana. She earned her Bachelors and Masters degrees from Dartmouth College. Being the only student from Lame Deer High School to receive an Ivy League education, she regularly returns as a motivational speaker for the youth. Spear has contributed to *The Journal,* a Dartmouth publication, as well as *A Cheyenne Voice, Native Sun News, LastRealIndians.com,* and *Native Max Magazine.* As an artist, Cinnamon regularly beads, sews, paints, but wishes she knew quillwork. Writing is her sanctuary, her freedom, but also her duty. As she flew back and forth between poverty and privilege (both states existing on and off the reservation), Spear realized that her super-exposed, bi-cultured hybrid state allowed her to teach the world about the Northern Cheyenne people, and likewise, to teach her people about the world.

Adrian L. Jawort, Northern Cheyenne, has been a journalist for some 12 very odd years. As well as writing for various indie newspapers, he's written for several nationally distributed publications that include Cowboys & Indians and Native Peoples magazines, and is a continual correspondent and columnist for Indian Country Today Media Network. When not writing articles, he also works construction like Jesus and hones his craft in creating the art of fiction and poetry. He also has a dark fantasy novel under his belt, *Moonrise Falling,* and is the founder of Off the Pass Press LLC which aims to find unconventional beauty in literature off the beaten path. Some say he writes to heal a broken heart and the ink droplets on the page represent years of tears, but he claims that's fanciful malarkey and it's simply a gratifying soul cleansing exercise that makes him feel more alive. So they say.

Luella N. Brien, Apsáalooké, graduated from The University of Montana School of Journalism in 2006, where she was the first student editor and contributor for UM's trailblazing reznetnews.org. A 2002 graduate of the Freedom Forum's American Indian Journalism Institute, Brien was also the president of the Native American Journalism Association's (NAJA) first student chapter, chartered in 2005. She's alumni of the prestigious Chips Quinn Scholars Program and the Associated Press's Diverse Voices Program, both aimed at increasing minority presence in the newsroom. After working stints at the Ravalli Republic and The Billings Gazette, she now serves her community as a communication arts instructor at Little Big Horn College in Crow Agency. Brien lives with her three children, who have taught her there are infinite ways to view the world.

Eric L. BigMan Brien is a member of the Crow (Apsáalooké) Tribe. He is the proud father of four beautiful and talented children. He credits his numerous teachers, Grandmother Beverly and sister Luella as those who have inspired him to write. When he is not writing he moonlights as an Elvis impersonator and enjoys reading religious tracks, travel brochures and medical pamphlets. He is fond of Carnivals and Cosplay, and describes being a member of the Crow Native American tribe as, "Swell."

Sterling HolyWhiteMountain grew up on the Blackfeet Reservation, where he lived the first part of his life according to the laws of the local basketball religion. He holds a BA in English Creative Writing from the University of Montana, a Masters in Creative Writing from the Iowa Writers' Workshop, and was a James C. McCreight Fiction Fellow at the University of Wisconsin. He is also the owner and founder of Rez Made, the new clothing company for reservation peoples and their relations. Currently he is working on a collection of novellas & stories, and is taking classes toward a BA in Native American Studies at the University of Montana. In his spare time he enjoys reading, conversations about art & aesthetics, following North American indigenous politics, and spending way too much time on various social media.

CPSIA information can be obtained
at www.ICGtesting.com
Printed in the USA
LVOW10s1841301017
554296LV00015B/1391/P